Made That Way

by

Susan Ketchen

OOLICHAN BOOKS
FERNIE, BRITISH COLUMBIA, CANADA
2010

Library and Archives Canada Cataloguing in Publication

Ketchen, Susan

Made that way / by Susan Ketchen.

ISBN 978-0-88982-270-2

I. Title.

PS8621.E893M33 2010   jC813'.6   C2010-907156-5

We gratefully acknowledge the financial support of the Canada Council for
the Arts, the British Columbia Arts Council through the BC Ministry of
Tourism, Culture, and the Arts, and the Government of Canada through
the Canada Book Fund, for our publishing activities.

Published by
Oolichan Books
P.O. Box 2278
Fernie, British Columbia
Canada V0B 1M0

www.oolichan.com

Printed in Canada on 100% post consumer recycled FSC-certified
paper.

Cover Photo by Isobel Springett, www.isobelspringett.com.

MIX
Paper from
responsible sources
FSC
www.fsc.org   FSC® C013916

For Mike

CHAPTER ONE

I am galloping. I'm riding a cross-country course, like the top riders do in the Olympics, and I only do in my dreams. I feel the wind on my face and the power of the horse beneath me. We head down a hill, which isn't easy without a saddle or bridle. I steer by shifting my balance and the horse responds as if he's part of me or I'm part of him, I can't say which.

At the bottom of the hill there's room for two strides, then there's a log, and then a pond. We're splashing through the pond when the scene changes—in an abrupt and disorienting way, like it does when I'm watching TV with my dad and he has the remote control channel-changer. Now a truck and horse trailer are crawling up my friend Kansas's driveway. The truck has Saskatchewan plates so I know this is my new horse arriving, the one Grandpa found for me. But I also know that I shouldn't be able to read the license plate from this far away, and that the truck is moving in slow motion, so even if I hadn't noticed before, this proves that I must be dreaming again, one of those lucid dreams where I know I'm dreaming and sometimes I can influence how things happen.

Then the truck transforms into my mom's car, which

explains its slow progress. My mom says her car is on its last legs. I have told her this is an inappropriate metaphor for a car but she says it all the time anyway.

Kansas is beside me, shaking her head. "Everyone knows you need at least a three-quarter-ton to pull a horse trailer," she says. "Especially a heavy old steel one like that."

The horse trailer is rusty and a window is open and hanging lop-sided from one hinge. I can see a shadow moving inside, and hear a bugled Ha Ha Ha which doesn't sound at all like a horse whinny. It sounds more like that stupid unicorn that wrecks so many of my dreams. I don't even believe in unicorns, so I get kind of annoyed when he barges into my night-life. Plus he's always grumpy and says things to upset me. Well, most of the time. Occasionally he's sensible.

I decide to try to make him sensible for this dream, though usually I have no control over what the unicorn does. Generally my control is limited to things like the clothes I'm wearing. I check out my feet. I'm wearing sandals, which Kansas does not approve of. She insists that anyone walking around her boarding stable has to wear boots, preferably with steel toes. She says you never know what's going to happen around horses. I concentrate and my sandals transform into my Ariat Junior Performer Paddock Boots.

Kansas still isn't happy. "Lord knows what we're going to find here," she says. "I really wanted to pick out the right horse for you, maybe next year, when your seat is established and your hands are steady. You could have leased Electra and taken lessons . . . ." She trails off in disgust. I've never heard Kansas talk this way before, but I've suspected for a long time that this is how she feels. I hate disappointing Kansas, but this isn't my fault. It's not even really Grandpa's fault. I think it's just life.

Kansas is right, I'm not ready. So I try to make the trailer disappear. I try to make the whole rig back away down the driveway, but it keeps on coming. There's more yelling from the trailer, and then a white nose with flaring nostrils appears at the open window. It's the unicorn alright. I try to make it brown, or bay with a white blaze and then in total desperation pink with sparkles like the stick ponies in Toys R Us, but nothing works.

The unicorn is trying to get his entire head out the window, but something keeps catching. I know it's his horn, or what's left of it. For some reason it's been getting shorter and shorter with every dream—I don't know why, and I sure don't want to ask him.

"What's with him?" says Kansas.

"His horn is caught," I mumble.

"His *what?*"

The unicorn pushes again, I hear something snap and his head is outside the window. There's a red patch in the middle of his forehead. Blood is running down his nose, down the side of the trailer, down the driveway. There's blood everywhere and that's when I make myself wake up.

I have my usual headache. Today is the day my new horse arrives so it would have been nice if, for a change, my skull didn't feel like it was going to explode, but no such luck.

Mom is tapping lightly on my door. "Wake up, Sugarplum. It's time for your injection."

My doctors tell me that I have Turner Syndrome. I'm missing an X chromosome, and my ovaries are atrophying even though I'm not even fifteen yet, and I'm short—really really short. The injection is Human Growth Hormone. If I don't take it I will never reach five feet. Not that this matters so much now. Getting to five feet used to be my entire reason for living, because that was the height I had to reach before Grandpa would buy me a horse. Now he's bought me one anyway, and my parents have gone along with it, probably because everyone has been overwhelmed with guilt for not noticing there was something seriously wrong with me since I was born. They even ignored me when I said that I didn't want my own horse right now, that I'm happy riding Electra, Kansas's lesson pony. Grandpa phoned last week and announced that he'd found the perfect horse for me back there in Saskatchewan and wanted to know how to ship it out. Grandpa doesn't always think things through properly. I think he's suffering from senile dementia. But I figured my parents would get involved and tell him to forget it, and instead they were all for it. They're too young for senile dementia, so I think it's just the guilt at work on them.

Now I feel guilty too. You'd think that maybe with missing a chromosome I might not have inherited the guilt gene, but somehow I did. I feel guilty about all the trouble people are going to for something I don't want. I feel guilty for letting down Kansas. But most of the time, when I feel guilty, it's about what I've done to my cousin, Taylor.

Mom opens my curtains. I sit on the side of my bed and peel back my nightshirt, then stare blearily at my puny thigh muscle.

"Mom, I don't like this."

"Honey, it's nothing, not even a little prick." She rips

open the packet for the alcohol swab. I catch a whiff of it and the pain increases in my forehead and then seeps around behind my ears.

"Mom, I have a headache. I always have a headache."

"You don't always have a headache, Sweetheart," says Mom swabbing my leg.

Okay, she's right, I'm exaggerating. I try to remember when the headaches started. I didn't have them at school last year, that's for sure. I had enough trouble at school without adding headaches to the list, what with everyone teasing me. Well, maybe not everyone. Logan Losino was nice. So the headaches must have started during the summer holidays.

"Maybe your riding helmet is too tight," says Mom. "Can you ask Kansas to check that for you? But I'll bet that today you're just excited about getting your new horse, aren't you, Honey? And you want to grow, don't you?" She positions the auto-injector over my thigh and presses the button to administer the dose. It stings. "There, you didn't even feel it, did you? Now I've got to go, Dad's already left." She kisses my cheek. "I love you, Sweetie. I wish I could be there with you today, but I'm fully booked. That new employee assistance contract I landed is keeping me so swamped." She shakes her head sadly but at the same time she has a smile on her face, as if there's something about being swamped that she likes. As if she doesn't really care if she's there when my horse arrives. Still, it's nice that she trusts Kansas. I know she's been struggling for months to build up her counselling practice, and I know she needs a new car. Plus we need money to pay for boarding my horse.

I sigh. Who am I to wreck her day?

"You be careful on your bike," says Mom from the doorway. "Have a good breakfast, and pack a lunch for yourself, you need to keep your strength up." Then even though she's out of time she lists all the nutritious things she's stocked in the kitchen that I can choose from when I pack my lunch. She goes on and on and when she starts working her way through all the yoghurt flavours I stop listening. I'm glad my mom is happy and that her practice is getting busy and that she's a conscientious parent who attends well to my nutritional needs. If she hadn't fed me so well since birth, maybe I'd be even shorter than I am now. For the most part I don't want her involved with my riding activities because she has a tendency to become too interested in my life and then offers lots of wacko opinions even if she doesn't know what she's talking about, like that horseback riding is an early adolescent phallic activity.

But still, this is an important day for me, and I'm nervous, and I'm not feeling well.

"Mom, do you think . . . "

"Oh lord," she says looking at her watch. "I have to go. Phone if you need me, any time. Leave a message, I'll call you back between sessions."

She whirls off down the hallway. I sit on the bed for a while. I hadn't had time to recover from that awful dream, and now I also have to recover from my mom, and my injection. I feel like Hurricane Katrina has swept through my bedroom . . . and my life.

Through my window I can hear Mom outside trying to start the car. The ignition whines and complains but eventually catches. I listen as her car rattles and wheezes into the distance.

I should be happy but I'm not. I should be more than

happy, I should be ecstatic and over the moon with joy. Instead I feel sick. I wish I was more like Kansas. Kansas says she's in pain all the time from some "riding adventures" but she never lets it get her down. She says pain is just a thing of the mind, and you have a choice to either get over it or stay in bed and eat bonbons, whatever they are.

The phone rings in the kitchen and I walk as quickly as I can to get it without jarring my head. It's Kansas. She's just heard from the driver of the shipping company. He's on the ferry with the horses. They'll be here in two hours. I should get over to the stable as soon as I can on my bike.

"Horses?" I say. "Grandpa sent me two?" One was bad enough. Two would be impossible.

"Oh no," says Kansas. "Didn't I tell you? Kelly Cleveland's horse is coming in the same trailer. They picked him up in Alberta on the way through. Everything worked out perfectly."

"You mean Dr. Cleveland?" I ask, and Kansas says yes. Dr. Cleveland is my psychiatrist and I like her a lot. She's the one who first suspected I had Turner Syndrome when my mom dragged me to see her because Mom thought I was a bisexual (it's a long story). Dr. Cleveland also said that there's nothing psychiatrically wrong with me unless "horse-nut" becomes an official clinical diagnosis. Dr. Cleveland was wearing Ariat paddock boots, so I knew right away she was a member of the herd, I knew she was a horsewoman, but I didn't know she was shipping her horse out from Alberta, and I didn't know she'd be boarding with Kansas. This is exciting news. This should make me even more ecstatically happy, and maybe it would if I didn't still have the stupid headache or hadn't had that stupid dream.

My mom has left a note for me on the kitchen table. I try to read it but I can't. Her handwriting is always impossible, but today it seems worse, even if I squint. It probably wasn't important. It probably wasn't anything she hasn't told me a million times already.

I grab a blueberry yoghurt from the fridge and rip off the foil cover, then stare at it. I know if I eat it I'll throw up. I take it to the bathroom and flush it down the toilet so mom doesn't find it in the garbage. Then I throw up anyway.

I decide there isn't much point in packing a lunch.

I have a quick shower and get dressed. I put on my breeches and my Ariat Junior Performer Paddock Boots even though I probably won't be riding today. Usually it makes me feel better to wear my riding clothes. But today nothing helps, even when I buckle on my riding helmet and hop on my bike. Somehow I know I'm doomed.

CHAPTER TWO

When I arrive, Kansas is raking the stable yard with one of her plastic mucking forks. The place is already immaculate, as it always is, but still she's raking. She even rakes over the line in the gravel left by my bike tires.

"Hey, Sylvia, that was quick." She picks up near-invisible pieces of hay and horse manure and deposits them in the wheelbarrow, though most of the bits are so small they fall through the tines of the fork before it gets a foot off the ground. Usually she is only this over-the-top fussy when Declan is on his way to shoe her horses, so I know she must be nervous. I hope it has nothing to do with me, I hope she's just nervous because Dr. Cleveland's horse is arriving, but this probably isn't the case.

She smiles at me but her lips are stiff, like they're made of skin-tone Styrofoam. "Pretty exciting, isn't it—your first horse arriving! And don't you look great!"

She's trying too hard. I can't disappoint her, so I nod, which makes my head hurt, but I'm not going to say anything because if I'm going to be a real horsewoman I have to learn to live with the pain. Kansas can usually tell when I'm not feeling right, but today she hardly looks me in the eye, and then she goes back to raking the gravel. She must be distracted too, like my mom but for different reasons. When I'm an adult, I hope I remember not to be distracted by anything, especially around young people who are feeling vulnerable.

I tell Kansas I'm going to check my horse's stall even though we both know it will already be perfect. I'm hoping I'll feel better if I'm out of the sun.

The barn is cool and dark and sharply scented from fresh shavings. The stall for my horse is clean and the water bucket is full. There's a flake of hay fluffed up in one corner on top of a patch of bare rubber matt. Unfortunately there's not a thing for me to do here, so I head out again, but before I leave the barn I notice that one of my bootlaces is loose, so I re-tie it and when I stand up everything goes fuzzy. I flip a bucket upside-down and sit on it just inside the main door. Pain is just a thing of the mind. I can deal with this.

Dr. Cleveland pulls up and parks beside Kansas's old truck. Dr. Cleveland drives a shiny silver-grey SUV with no dints or scratches in it, kind of like my dad's, though his SUV is black because he says that's a business-like colour. When she opens the door I catch a glimpse of a console that looks like something out of a spaceship. I didn't think women cared about automotive stuff—Kansas says her truck has purely functional value, and my mom's car doesn't even have that. So I thought having fancy vehicles was more a guy thing. As usual I'm left thinking I have a lot to learn about adult life.

Dr. Cleveland leaps out, looking around wildly. "Are they here yet? Did I miss the trailer?" She hasn't done up her shirt properly, so the buttons are misaligned.

I have never seen her like this. In her office she is

subdued and dignified. Now she looks like a very tall kid with Attention Deficit Hyperactivity Disorder.

Kansas says, "I didn't think you'd be coming until after work."

"I booked the afternoon off. I said there was a family emergency—which there is of course."

Kansas rakes away the tire marks left by Dr. Cleveland's car. "I could have handled this for you, Kelly," she says.

"Are you kidding?" says Dr. Cleveland. "I wouldn't miss this for the world." She spies me sitting in the doorway to the barn, waves and says hi. "Exciting day, eh Sylvia?" But she turns and pops open the back hatch before I can answer. She's distracted too. Maybe being distracted is part of being an adult. Maybe it's something they teach you at university.

The back of Dr. Cleveland's vehicle is cram-packed with gear. I don't know how she's going to stuff it all in her locker in the tack room. Kansas must be wondering the same thing. She's stopped raking and is staring at what could almost be a small tack shop on wheels. Without even standing up I can see a stack of three saddle pads in different shades of blue. In plastic bags beside them are perfectly coordinated polo wraps for her horse's legs.

Dr. Cleveland smiles sheepishly for Kansas. "I have matchy-matchy disease."

"So I see," says Kansas.

"Sadly, it's an untreatable genetic disorder," says Dr. Cleveland.

"That is very sad," says Kansas.

I know they're kidding around, but given the fact that they both know that I have a genetic disorder I'd have thought they'd be more sensitive. I guess they're too excited to be worrying about my feelings right now.

"It's linked to a compulsive shopping gene," continues Dr. Cleveland, "and the shopping-as-recreation reductase enzyme."

"I knew that," says Kansas.

Dr. Cleveland leans into her vehicle and drags forward another armful of gear.

That's when I hear the air brakes out on the roadway. I rise slowly to my feet, keeping my head low as long as possible. The rest seems to have helped, my headache has died down to a dull background kind of pain that I should be able to ignore. It's more like a toothache now than an exploding head kind of thing.

When I look up Dr. Cleveland is rubbing the back of her head with her hand. I guess she banged it on the hatch by straightening up too fast when she heard the truck.

I walk over and stand beside Kansas, and the three of us watch the truck and trailer roll up the driveway. It's nothing like my dream. The trailer is huge; I bet it could hold at least six horses. And it's being towed by one of those transport trucks that haul semi-trailers. Even in my horse magazines I've never seen such a big rig for horses.

"Oh good," says Kansas. "They had an air-conditioned ride."

"It wouldn't have mattered—Braveheart is a good traveller," says Dr. Cleveland. "What about your horse, Sylvia, has he had much trailering experience?"

I have something suddenly wrong with my throat and I can't talk, so Kansas answers for me. "We don't know," she says ominously but Dr. Cleveland doesn't react, which seems odd to me, even if she is distracted, because like my mom she is still a helping professional. My mom would never miss the opportunity to delve into some psychological puzzle.

"I am so excited!" says Dr. Cleveland. "Do you think he'll remember me, Kansas? I haven't seen him for three months!"

"Oh, I expect so," says Kansas.

"You'll love Braveheart, everybody does," says Dr. Cleveland. "He's a real gentleman, a very honest horse."

"Honest?" I manage to say. "What does that mean?"

"Well . . . ," says Dr. Cleveland, but then grinds to a halt.

"It means he's obedient and has a good work ethic and makes an effort to learn what you're teaching him," says Kansas.

"Everyone should have an honest horse like Braveheart," says Dr. Cleveland.

"I know," says Kansas. Again I can hear that ominous tone. She's holding something back. Then she says, "Sylvia's grandfather found this horse for her." And I realize she's talking in code for Dr. Cleveland's benefit, and she's trying not to criticize my grandpa. My dream was right. Kansas wanted to pick out the right horse for me. She must think this is totally crazy, getting an unknown horse from thousands of miles away. I can feel my headache rebuilding.

"Braveheart is my heart horse," says Dr. Cleveland dreamily.

I look up at her. I wonder if she's on drugs. My dad says that it's not uncommon for medical professionals to become addicted to prescription medications because they receive free samples all the time from the pharmaceutical companies. Dr. Cleveland smiles down at me briefly, then returns her attention to the truck.

The truck stops in front of us in the yard. It's a huge looming burgundy thing with lots of shiny metal trim pieces. The engine shuts off then pings as it cools down. Kansas rubs her palms on her pants, and Dr. Cleveland bounces on her toes and makes chirping noises. This is the best day of my life, I tell myself over and over. Pain is a thing of the mind. Be happy. Be happy.

We are lined up by the driver's door, and have to wait forever as he makes some notations on a clipboard, finds his ball cap, and finally finally climbs down from the cab. He refers to the clipboard.

"I have two deliveries here. One for a Dr. K. Cleveland. The other for Sylvia Forrester. Have I got the right place?"

I can't say anything and Dr. Cleveland sounds like she has a squeaky toy stuck in her throat, so Kansas has to answer. "Right place," she says, then introduces herself as the barn owner. When she finishes, she glances my way then peers at me more closely. "Are you okay?" she whispers, "You're white as a ghost." She looks to Dr. Cleveland, probably hoping for an on-the-spot medical consultation, just as a loud bang reverberates from the trailer.

"Sounds like they want to get out," says Dr. Cleveland.

"Might as well," says the driver. He leans the clipboard on the step beside the cab, pulls a pair of leather gloves from his hip pocket and slips them on.

He lowers the ramp at the side of the trailer.

"There he is," says Kelly. "Hi, Braveheart. I'm here! Remember me?" She is waving and cooing. A large chestnut head with a wide white blaze stretches into view.

He's wearing a leather shipping helmet. An impatient leg reaches forward, wrapped to the knee in blue padded shipping boot.

I stretch onto my tiptoes, trying to see past Braveheart, but then I lose my balance and Kansas grabs my elbow.

"Can you see him?" I ask.

"Not yet," says Kansas.

"We'll unload the big guy first," says the driver. "What is he, 16.3?"

"17.2," says Dr. Cleveland breathlessly.

"Jesus," says Kansas.

The driver climbs the ramp, clips a lead rope onto Braveheart's leather halter and drops the chest bar. He takes the horse forward a step and barely manages to check him at the top of the ramp. "Can't get away from him soon enough, can you, fella?" he says, as if a horse as big as Braveheart could be scared of anything. He leads the horse down into the yard and hands the rope to Dr. Cleveland.

"Oh, Braveheart," she says. She wipes her shirtsleeve across her eyes. "It is so good to see you again." She reaches a hand up to stroke his neck which is upright and rigid. He doesn't even know she's there. He is staring across the yard to the horses out in the paddock, and bellows a welcome. Hambone answers with a loud whinny, then gathers up his mares and gallops them to the far end of the pasture. Braveheart wheels around Dr. Cleveland in a tight excited circle. Kansas puts her arm around my shoulders and backs me out of range, then we stand there together, watching and waiting.

"That is a big horse," I murmur.

"That is a very big horse," says Kansas. "Of course they

always grow a hand or two when they're excited. At least I hope that's what's happened here."

A thin bugling sound wafts from the darkness of the far side of the trailer. It's nothing like the calls the other horses are making.

"What's that?" says Kansas. "It sounds like something from the alien bar in *Star Wars*."

"Oh no," I say, then clamp a hand across my mouth.

"What?" says Kansas.

The driver ascends the ramp for his second passenger. If I could talk I would tell him to close the door and take the horse back where he found him. But I can't talk. It's all I can do to stay on my feet. I'm sure any second now I'm going to throw up again. I can't even run away because Kansas has me held tight against her side. I'm trapped.

The driver reaches forward with the lead and drops the chest bar. Unlike Braveheart, my horse isn't so eager to leave the trailer. The driver pats him on the neck and tells him to step forward, but when this doesn't work he takes a length of chain out of his pocket. I can't see what he's doing, but I've watched Kansas slip a chain over Hambone's nose when he's been difficult, so I figure the driver's doing the same thing here. My poor pony.

"Thought you'd change your mind," the driver says.

When they get to the top of the ramp I won't look at my horse's head. I decide to focus on his legs. Big mistake. Immediately I can see there's something wrong. Even I can see it, and I know next to nothing. The horse is pointing his right front foot, trying to keep his weight off it. When the driver asks him to step forward to the ramp he leads with his left front and short-steps with the right. I tell myself maybe

I'm imagining this, maybe nothing is wrong, maybe some horses are gimpy walking off trailers, but then Kansas says, "Oh dear."

The ground comes up in front of me and suddenly I'm on my knees, throwing up in the dirt.

I hear the driver lead the horse the rest of the way down the ramp and Kansas steps away from me to take the lead rope. "Not what she was expecting?" says the driver. "He's not a bad little guy." I look up just in time to see the horse lunge forward and bite the driver on the arm. The horse hangs on like a pit bull until the driver cuffs him across the ears with his free hand.

"Holy crap," says the driver. He turns his back and doubles up over his arm.

I rock back and sit cross-legged in the dirt, staring at Kansas's feet and four black hooves at the end of four grey legs. I know I should stand up and move out of the way, but even if I could stand, this would mean I'd have to take a closer look at my new horse and I don't want to. I've seen enough. When he lunged at the driver I saw the patch of hair missing from his forehead. I heard his weird whinny. I know what I have here.

I can hear Electra, Hambone and Photon letting loose in the paddock, the air and ground vibrating with the impact of their hooves as they gallop from one end of the field to another. Braveheart is yelling from his stall and Dr. Cleveland is calling from the barn doorway. "Hey, Kansas, could you give me a hand getting him out of his shipping boots, he's a bit excited, I can usually manage him on his own, but—What's going on out here?"

CHAPTER THREE

Kansas insists on calling my mom, even though Dr. Cleveland says I'm probably just anxious. Of course I didn't mention about the headache, because we're all horsewomen, and horsewomen don't give in to pain, or even talk about it unless they absolutely have to. Maybe I am just anxious. But then I have a lot to be anxious about if I'm now the owner of a unicorn.

My mom can't leave work. She says she'll call my dad.

I hear his SUV pull up, skidding in the gravel, leaving ruts I'm sure. He and Kansas already don't get along all that well, and this isn't going to help. He doesn't close his door or remove the keys from the ignition, I can hear the warning chime all the way from the tack room where I'm sitting on a stool with an ice pack on the back of my neck (this was Kansas's idea).

"Are you okay, Peewee?" says Dad. He crouches in front of me and plops a hand on my shoulder. "Did you fall off your horse? I'll kill the bloody thing."

"Dad, no, I'm fine. I just threw up. Dr. Cleveland thinks it's from anxiety."

He stands up. "Anxiety? Your mom didn't say anything about that. I thought you'd been hurt. I left a meeting with . . . "

For some strange reason my eyes are filling with tears, and before I can hide my face, Dad notices. "Oh, never mind," he says, and puts a hand on my head. "As long as you're okay."

Kansas steps in beside him. "I didn't think she should ride her bike home. She kind of fainted."

"I didn't faint. And I don't want to go home yet." I get to my feet, and stuff the ice pack back into the freezer compartment of the little fridge, which gives me some time to get my act back together. I don't know what came over me. I turn to face them. "I'm fine now. Really."

Kansas is leaning against the door jamb. She's drying her arms on her t-shirt. She's been scrubbing water buckets and her sleeves are pushed up onto her shoulders. She has more muscles in her arms than I have in my legs. "You have lots of time to get to know your new pony," she tells me. "It doesn't all have to happen today." There's a smudge of dirt on her face and a clump of her hair has escaped from the broad blue elastic holding her pony tail. Instead of her usual paddock boots, she's wearing her work boots which I know have steel toes, this must have been in honour of the new horses arriving, and she's tucked her jeans haphazardly into the tops. The laces aren't tied, which kind of defeats the other safety precautions as far as I'm concerned, but what do I know? My dad, on the other hand, is wearing his good beige trousers and white dress shirt and gold and blue striped tie and there's not a wrinkle or crease or smudge anywhere. It's as though he has an invisible protective shield around himself, because I know I can't walk near the barn without attracting a layer of dirt.

"Come on, Munchkin, I'll take you home," he says.

He holds out an arm for me. He wants to usher me to

his car, and partly I want to go with him, I want to fold against him and be taken care of, but also I notice he's calling me Peewee and Munchkin again, and if it's time he stopped treating me like a child then maybe I have to stop acting like one. So I squint at him, and am just about to say something that Mom would probably call defiant, when Kansas says, "Why don't you take him to meet your pony, *Sylvia*?" She puts a nice stress on my name for me.

I take Dad's hand. Maybe if I'm holding on to him it won't be so bad looking at the unicorn. I lead him down the alleyway and Kansas tags along behind us.

Dad and I peer over the half-door into the darkness at the back of the stall where my new "pony" is trying to make himself invisible. Dad stands close so I can smell his after-shave. I warn him not to lean on the door or he'll get his shirt dirty. I have to stand on an upturned bucket because Kansas has asked me not to climb on the doors, she says it's bad for the hinges. I don't mind. Kansas and I both know this is temporary, and that once the growth hormone starts to work I'll be able to see over the doors like everyone else in the world who is more than six years old.

"Is he supposed to look like that?" says Dad.

"He'll be fine," says Kansas, unconvincingly. "He's probably shell-shocked from the traveling. He'll likely settle in, but we need to give him a few days."

I can tell that Kansas isn't happy, but I'm not going to tell her that I know what the problem is, and that it's not going to go away, because instead of a horse or even a pony, I have a unicorn. She won't notice for a while, what with the horn missing, and also because he's grey and not white like everyone thinks unicorns are supposed to be. But

I know that in horses, if they're grey when they're younger, they gradually turn white. And it's probably the same with unicorns.

Dad extends his arm into the stall and twiddles his fingers, saying, "Hey horsey."

Kansas reaches over top of me, grabs my dad's forearm and draws it out of the stall. When she lets go I see a mucky brown handprint on my dad's white shirtsleeve.

"There was an incident with the driver. The horse may not like men. We're not sure yet," Kansas explains.

"An incident?" says Dad vaguely. He brushes at the dirt mark on his sleeve but it doesn't move.

"He bit the driver," I say, trying to distract Dad from how Kansas wrecked his shirt. "He was like a pit bull."

Probably this wasn't the right thing to say. Dad looks narrow-eyed at Kansas, who shrugs.

"This horse isn't safe," says Dad.

Kansas blinks. "Of course he's not safe. He's an animal. If you want safe, ride a bicycle."

Dad looks down at me. His eyes are pink around the edges.

"Dad, I'll be fine." And to show him how confident I am, I cross my arms on the top of the stall door and rest my chin on the back of my wrists. I am feeling a bit better. While I was waiting for Dad to arrive, Dr. Cleveland gave me some diluted Gatorade in case I was dehydrated. Then Kansas made me eat some of her peanut butter and honey sandwich. Miraculously it stayed down. And pain is a thing of the mind.

But then Dad takes another look into the back of the stall and says, "What happened to his head?" And my heart stops.

Kansas says, "Some horses are born with big heads like that, they don't all have elegant little faces like Electra's." She says it like she's trying to make a point about how this whole horse purchase thing was not a good idea.

"I mean the place on his forehead where he doesn't have any fur," says Dad.

At least there isn't blood pouring out of it, like in my dream. I decide not to mention this.

"Oh that. Sorry, Sylvia," says Kansas. "I shouldn't have said . . . anyway, it looks like he scraped himself in the trailer, that sort of thing happens all the time." She doesn't say anything more for a while, then adds, "His eye is nice though, large and dark."

It took her long enough to come up with something nice to say about him.

"And his ears are nice and large too," Dad adds.

Kansas makes a kind of gargling sound.

"What's wrong with his coat?" I ask, because I actually like his ears and don't want to hear that there's something wrong with them, but on the other hand there's definitely something unusual about his coat. Kansas hums. She's probably trying to think of the least serious possible explanation so I don't worry. This is the sort of thing my parents do to me and I hate it, even today when I'm feeling weak in the knees. I want to know the truth. "I mean, here we are in August," I say, "and it almost looks like he's still got his winter coat."

Kansas sighs. "Well, it is a little coarse. Could be malnourished. Could be Cushings. Could be a bunch of things. Maybe he's part Shetland pony, who knows? How're you feeling?"

"Oh I'm fine," I lie, because I know she's trying to change the subject. The headache has come back full blast but I am not going to let her treat me like a baby or an invalid like everyone else does.

Kansas tells us she's going to bring Electra in from the field and put her in the stall next to my horse to give him some company. She says that should help him settle in faster, because horses are herd animals.

I'm not so sure that unicorns are herd animals, but I suppose we'll find out soon enough. I watch him at the back of the stall, his head down, eyes half-closed. He doesn't look very happy. Maybe he has a headache too. I look up at my dad to see if he's noticed, but he's watching Kansas disappear up the driveway, the halter and lead rope slung over her back and a carrot sticking out of her bum pocket. Standing on the bucket, I'm about level with my dad's shoulder, and I watch him in profile. I think he's very handsome, even though he's old. I like the way his hair curls out over the back of his shirt collar. I like how I can see the pin prick spots where his beard is growing in despite the fact that he shaves every morning. I like the way he smells.

"Look," says Dad, "I have a couple of calls to make. I'll be in the car. I'll put your bike in the back. You come out when you're finished and I'll drive you home." He pats me on the bum and leaves.

Dr. Cleveland exits Braveheart's stall with an armload of shipping boots and the blue summer sheet the horse had been wearing to keep off the dust. Dr. Cleveland is glowing. At least someone is happy, but it makes everything worse, because this is how I should be feeling and no matter how hard I try, I can't.

She stops beside me and peers down into my horse's stall. "Oh," she says.

"He needs some time to settle in," I tell her.

For a long time she's quiet and then she says, "I always loved grays."

She doesn't sound convinced. It's as though she can't understand if she always loved grays then why doesn't she like this one.

There's a long silence. Dr. Cleveland shifts her load of gear from one arm to the other. "You'd seen pictures of him, before you bought him?" she asks.

I know what she's getting at. If I didn't know she was totally distracted by having her own horse arrive, I'd be worried she thought I was plain stupid. I guess I have to make allowances for her, like I seem to have to make allowances for all adults, but it's very disappointing. "My grandpa bought him for me, from a friend of his in Saskatchewan. He wanted him to be a surprise."

"Hmmm," says Dr. Cleveland. "Does he have a name?"

Of course Grandpa had told me his name, but it had flown out of my head as soon as I saw him, because it clearly was not a name for a unicorn. "Brooklyn," I say.

"Like the bridge," says Dr. Cleveland.

My stomach turns over and I look at her in horror. "A bridge?"

"Brooklyn Bridge," says Dr. Cleveland, heading off to the locker room, not noticing a thing.

CHAPTER FOUR

I'm dreaming, and I know I'm dreaming, but I'm exhausted from the previous day and don't have the energy to control where the dream goes. I hope nothing goes wrong or that if something does go badly I will have the energy to wake myself up. At first everything's fine. I'm cantering along a trail and we pop over a small drop jump. Then we're going a bit too fast, so I sit up like Kansas has told me to and slow the motion in my back. The horse responds by dropping to a walk and we mosey along, enjoying the countryside.

I know I'm dreaming because Kansas won't let me jump yet. When I have lessons on Electra we only do flatwork. Dressage is Kansas's passion. I don't mind doing it if it's going to make me a better jumper rider, but sometimes it does get boring, which is probably why I never bother to dream about it.

Suddenly the horse disappears, and I'm on my feet.

The unicorn is limping beside me. There's a scab on his forehead where his horn used to be. He says, "Did you hear what the driver said? *Not a bad little guy?*"

I scuff my feet in the dirt. Fortunately I'm wearing my paddock boots. Sometimes in the past I've been wearing ballet slippers, which are the sort of thing my cousin Taylor likes to wear because she is a dance-nut the same way I am a horse-nut. This footwear switching is only one way things can become very mixed up in my dreams. Apparently there are rules to lucid dreaming. Sometimes I break them accidentally and then crazy things happen. The main thing is that I'm not supposed to build bridges between worlds by mentioning the name of someone from the real world while I'm in the dream world. The last time I made a mistake, suddenly Taylor was with me in the dream, and the unicorn followed her in because unicorns used to be her spiritual protectors. She had pictures of them all over her bedroom. But this particular unicorn wasn't very nice, and he had very pointy teeth that scared Taylor out of her mind. Her life has been ruined by my error—she's had to remove all the unicorn decorations from her room and she's still looking for a new guardian for her soul.

I look around nervously, hoping that thinking about Taylor won't be enough of a bridge to draw her into the dream.

"I need to rest for a moment," says the unicorn.

We are under a large tree. I take a seat on a curve of root and stare at my boots. I wish I could ask the unicorn why my new "horse" was named after a bridge, because it's really bothering me, but obviously I can't.

"I don't know about those drugs you're getting," says the unicorn.

"The growth hormone? I need that for the Turner Syndrome or I won't grow."

"What's so bad about being short? I have a good life and never grew over fifteen hands."

"A good life? You're grumpy all the time."

"I am not."

"And Dr. Cleve…" I stop myself just in time. "My psychiatrist said it generally helped people psychologically to break the five-foot barrier."

"Generally speaking. Not always. Not if it means you have a headache every day until your epiphyses close over."

"My what?"

"You know. Until the growth plates have fused at the end of your long bones. Until you reach bone age fourteen."

"I thought you said you didn't know anything about this? You said you reported on the general spiritual picture."

"I've been reading up on it."

"Oh right, now you're a unicorn that reads. I suppose you have high speed internet access back home in your mountain cave as well."

"Sylvia . . . ," he says, using that warning tone that adults are so fond of and drives me crazy.

I launch myself from the root. "Do not talk to me like that! Do not treat me like a child. I am so sick of this." I glare at him and barely restrain myself from punching him in the nose. I decide to hurt him another way. "What happened to your horn?"

He turns away. I can see his face in profile, which makes the absence more obvious.

"And why can you call me by my name and I can't call you anything? Is that fair?" I can feel my frustration building. I know I'm going to cry and when that starts I'll wake up. I don't have much time left. "What kind of spiritual creature are you anyway?"

His head sweeps back slowly and he considers me with deep dark sad eyes.

"Flawed, just like the rest of you," he says.

I throw my arms around his neck, hold him and sob.

Of course this wakes me up.

It's still early.

I ease myself out of bed, hoping not to give myself a headache right away. I part the curtains and look out the window for a while. I can tell it's going to be another hot day, there's not a cloud anywhere.

I can hear my parents chattering away to each other in the bathroom. I wonder how it is that they never seem to run out of things to talk about despite sleeping with each other all night and having lived with each other for a couple of decades.

I stand in front of my mirror. I sleep in a long t-shirt. My mom used to buy me nighties with frills and cutesy pictures on them, and I thought this was my only option until I met Kansas. I helped her fold her laundry once. All she ever sleeps in is t-shirts.

I roll my sleeves up over my shoulders and flex my biceps. A small bulge forms, about the size of half a golf ball. Kansas says not to worry, that doing barn chores and learning to ride will develop all sorts of muscles.

I turn sideways to the mirror and pull in my stomach and puff out my chest muscles.

That's when Mom peeks her head in the door. "Oh, you're up already, Pumpkin?" she says. And before I can answer she comes in, shuts the door behind her and sits on the edge of my bed. She has my injection in her hand but she's lost interest. "You know, Sweetie, there's no reason you can't wear a padded bra . . . until the medication starts working."

"What?" I say. Then I look back to my reflection in the mirror. "Mom, no. I was checking my *muscles*."

"No one would need to know," says Mom. "Auntie Sally says the best place to go is that lingerie shop on Fifth Street."

"You talked to Auntie Sally?" I am so mortified.

"She went there for Erika," says Mom, as if this would make me feel better. Erika is ten.

She's relentless. I do what I have to do to get her off my case, though in a way it's too late already because my headache has come back. "I'll think about it," I say. I sit on the bed beside her.

"Oh good," she says. "Can you phone Grandpa before you go to the barn today and let him know everything worked out fine yesterday? We should have called him last night but we forgot."

"Okay," I say. I'd rather not get into a discussion with her about whether or not everything really worked out fine yesterday.

She waggles the injector in front of me. "I have your medication."

"Mom, I have a headache."

"Again?"

Finally she's heard me. Finally I have her complete attention. "Still. I always have a headache. Yesterday I threw up. It's from the growth hormone."

"Now what makes you think .that, Sweetie? They told us there should be no side effects. And didn't Dr. Cleveland say yesterday that she thought you were just anxious? She should know."

I stare at my thigh and wonder if I can say that a unicorn in my dreams told me the headaches were from the medication. My mom would never buy it. I wouldn't buy it myself, except it makes such perfect sense.

I feel the sting on my thigh as she administers the dose. "I'm sure it's just all the excitement, Honey."

"Mom, it's more than that."

She cocks her head as though she's considering a new possibility, and for a brief moment I feel some hope, but then she launches into her usual sort of thing. She even has a different tone of voice, as though she's being interviewed by Oprah. "Well, you've never struck me as the type, but perhaps it's because I've been too close to you. Perhaps you do have an anxiety disorder . . . ." And her eyebrows pinch together as if she's mentally reviewing all the psychology textbooks she studied at university.

I groan. "Mom, no…"

"Oh you're right, I shouldn't have said *disorder*," she says. "That makes it sound terrible, that's why we try not to use labels, because they're pathologizing. And really, Sweetheart, anxiety is something that people can learn to manage. In fact I could teach you some terrific relaxation and visualization exercises. We can start tonight. It'll be fun! Now I've got to go, your dad's still here, he's in the shower." She kisses my cheek. "I love you, Pumpkin. Have a great day. Don't worry, you'll be fine—I promise."

I close my eyes. Why do adults have to be such morons? She *promises*? Obviously I'm on my own with this one. Tonight I'll do an in-depth search about growth hormone and side effects on Google. Google is usually reliable.

After I hear Mom's car clank off down the road, I throw on a sweater and drag myself to the kitchen. I phone Grandpa and he answers, breathing hard, on the eighth ring.

"Hi Grandpa. It's me, Sylvia."

"Hey Pipsqueak. What's new with you?"

As usual I'm unsure whether Grandpa is kidding or showing more signs of senile dementia. "Brooklyn got here yesterday," I tell him.

"Well how is he? Do you like him?"

"He bit the driver."

Grandpa clears his throat. "What does . . . er . . . Dakota think of that?"

"You mean Kansas. She's not sure. She says I have to be careful around him and give him time to settle in."

"That's good advice. Do you like him?"

"I think so." It's not so much that I'm lying as that I'm being kind. Grandpa has been very generous and I don't want to hurt his feelings. "Grandpa, do you know what breed he is? Kansas was wondering if maybe he was part Shetland pony, because his coat is kind of long, and because he isn't as tall as we were expecting."

"I don't know, Pipsqueak. I'll see if Travis knows, but he kept a lot of horses and now he's stuck in extended care. His son and I haven't been able to find all his records yet. He left things in an awful mess, not that I'm blaming him—how was he to know he was going to fall and break his hip? And who wants to be spending their precious time with paperwork? Life's too short for that. You need to be out there living it up enjoying things while you can. That's my advice to you, Pips."

"Okay, Grandpa." There's some crackling and buzzing down the line between us. I can't think of what else to say.

"Some of Travis's horses were imported from Europe," says Grandpa. "I'll keep looking through his files, how's that?"

"Thanks, Grandpa."

"And take your time," says Grandpa. "You don't need to rush anything. Give the horse a chance. Give yourself a chance. Everything will be fine."

"Erk," I say.

"You okay, Pipsqueak?"

"I have a headache. I think it's from the growth hormone."

"What does the doctor say?"

"I'm not scheduled to see the pediatrician for another two weeks. I could go see our family doctor, Dr. Destrie, but he would only say I have allergies. That's all he ever says, even when Stephanie had Chlamydia." Stephanie is my cousin too. She's Taylor's older sister, and Erika is the youngest. Taylor has warned me about Dr. Destrie, though my mom thinks he's super.

Grandpa isn't saying anything. Maybe he doesn't know what Chlamydia is either; I had to look it up the first time Taylor told me about it.

"That's a bacteria," I tell him.

"Of course it is," says Grandpa. He clears his throat. "You know, Pipsqueak, what I said about living it up and enjoying life while you can . . . well, there are limits."

"Okay," I say uncertainly. I don't know where this is going all of a sudden.

"When I was young . . . ." He has to stop for a bout of coughing. I hope he isn't getting pneumonia. This is how my dad says most old people die.

"Grandpa, are you okay?"

"Oh hell," he says. "What were we talking about? Never mind. And I shouldn't have said hell. What do I know? Let me know how it goes with the horse."

"Okay, Grandpa. And thank you for sending him," I say, but as usual Grandpa has hung up before I finish.

I turn around and Dad is watching me. His hair is wet from the shower. His eyes are kind of buggy. "You were telling Grandpa about Chlamydia?" he says.

He sounds so perplexed that I figure he doesn't know what it is either.

"It's a bacteria," I tell him.

"I know that," says Dad. "How do you know about it?" He's making such a big deal of this. "Stephanie had it. Dr. Destrie thought she had an allergic reaction to fabric softener. It's an STD," I tell him, because that's how Mom talks about these things—very matter of factly, preferably with acronyms. His Adam's apple bobbles up and down. I think it's time I changed the subject. "Dad, do you think I might have an anxiety disorder?"

"Jesus Christ," says Dad.

I decide to ignore this. "Because Mom thinks my headaches might be from anxiety, but I think they're from the growth hormone." Surely I can get someone on my side about this issue.

"I don't know, Shorty," he says. He hasn't called me Shorty in a long long time so I know he's exasperated. He checks his watch. "Shit," he says.

"Dad!"

He apologizes.

"And you said you wouldn't call me Shorty any more."

He puts his great big hand on top of my head. His face looks so sad, I regret reminding him. "I'm sorry, Sylv. I'm really sorry. I'll try harder. It's just I'm so busy right now, and I'm stressed about work, the economy's a mess, all those sub-prime mortgages . . . ."

- 41 -

CHAPTER FIVE

I cook a piece of toast and smear it with extra-crunchy peanut butter, but can't eat it. I know if I put it in my mouth I'll throw up again. Last night I somehow managed to eat dinner so maybe I'll have enough nourishment on board to take me through the morning. I grab an apple from the refrigerator and cut it into thin slices and put all but one of them in a zip-lock bag in my backpack. The extra slice I slip between my teeth and suck it carefully, drawing out the juice and swallowing a teeny bit at a time.

The phone rings, startling me into chewing and swallowing. I'm spluttering as I say hello.

"Sylvia? Is that you? You sound funny. It's me, Taylor. How'd it go yesterday? Did your horse arrive?"

Miraculously the apple stays down in my stomach where it's supposed to be. "Yeah," I say.

"And . . . ? You don't sound very excited. Is he okay? What's he look like? "

I'm reluctant to tell Taylor that the new pony has a striking resemblance to the unicorn that I dream about, or to any unicorn for that matter. "He's small and grey," I say.

Fortunately this is enough to satisfy Taylor, who is no more a horse-person than she is a unicorn-person any more.

"Oh," she says. "Well, I have some news too. I have decided on the new motif for my bedroom. I'm going to do angels."

"Angels?"

"They're perfect. They like to dance and they're a form of spirituality I can take forward with me into adulthood, because lots of people believe in angels."

I can well-imagine Taylor's room converted to a shrine for angels, with fluttery wings, gauzy fabric and sparkles strewn everywhere. "Sounds good, Taylor. I'm glad you found something finally to replace . . . you know what."

"My mom and I are going to the wallpaper store today. I'm so excited!"

I try to feel excited too but can't. I should be even more excited than Taylor because Taylor is only getting new wallpaper and curtains, and I have a new unicorn.

"I have to go!" says Taylor. "But I just had to tell you my news. Hope you have a great day!"

I have a shower, and afterwards stand barefoot against the edge of my bedroom door. I put my Pony Club manual on my head and then check my height against the measurement I took two days ago. I know I'm not supposed to check this often, I know the medication takes several months to make significant changes, but I can't help myself. Today there is no change, unless I cheat and slant the book, and what's the point of that?

I dress, grab my backpack, hop on my bike and pedal off to see Kansas. And Brooklyn, I remind myself. Brooklyn Bridge. I shake my head, which makes it hurt more and also makes my vision kind of blurry.

I pedal more gently and remember what the unicorn said in my last dream. What is so bad about being short?

Sure, the kids at school tease me, but if they didn't tease me about being short they'd tease me about something else. Kansas isn't very tall—she's over five feet, but no where near as tall as Dr. Cleveland who doesn't seem happier for it. If being tall was so important, you'd think that Dr. Cleveland would be ecstatically happy all the time. It's not that she's unhappy, she's just kind of subdued most of the time, though not yesterday of course.

I pedal and think. I imagine being back at school and being a horse-owner. Even Amber and Topaz should take me more seriously because of this. It's not like owning a new kitten. I am responsible for a very large animal. Soon I will be competing and jumping huge fences and undertaking death-defying acts of bravery. I will be a person to contend with instead of a shrimp with funny ears.

By the time I reach Kansas's driveway I'm feeling downright pumped. I decide I'll find a way of getting off the growth hormone. I'll stay short, and everything will be fine. Maybe I've just imagined everything about Brooklyn. Maybe he's not a unicorn, or even part-unicorn. Maybe he's an exotic pony imported originally from Europe. He had a rough trip from Saskatchewan, and all he needs is some time. Instead of looking up growth hormone tonight on Google I can investigate unusual pony breeds. I'll find something that looks like him somewhere.

But then I arrive at the barn and see that Brooklyn is in the wash rack. Kansas is beside him with the hose, trickling water over his right front leg. She doesn't look happy at all. And I remember thinking Brooklyn looked lame when he came off the trailer.

"It's nothing," she says. "He's a bit touchy on this foot,

and there might be some heat in the pastern. It could be an abscess. His feet are terrible. They've been neglected. Declan is coming." Her expression changes momentarily when she says Declan's name, a small smile comes to her lips, but then she looks back at Brooklyn and a scowl takes over.

I'm frozen astride my bike. Right front. Brooklyn has the same sore foot as the unicorn. I feel a swell coming up from my stomach and swallow hard.

"Don't fret, Sylvia. This isn't a big deal. He'll be fine. We'll just have to start slow. Put away your bike and you can help me."

I prop my bike against the back wall of the barn and when I come back Declan's truck is rolling up the driveway. He turns around in the yard and backs to the doorway of the barn. I watch Kansas's face transform when Declan climbs out of the cab. It goes all soft and warm and gooey. The outer corners of her eyes go down and her head tilts off to one side like she's got water in one ear.

"Hey, Declan, thanks for coming so quickly," she says.

"I was in the area," he says. I know he's lying.

"This is Sylvia's new pony." She puts extra emphasis for some reason on the word *pony*. Could she know? "I think he has an abscess," says Kansas.

I can't understand why Kansas is cold-hosing the leg if Brooklyn has an abscess. When Hambone had an abscess Kansas soaked the foot in warm water and Epsom salts. According to my Pony Club manual cold hosing would make sense if there was an injury to the fetlock joint, but if that was what Kansas was worried about then why did she call Declan? I look from Kansas to Declan and back again. Sometimes people, even smart people that I like, seem to do stupid things. This is terribly frustrating, because I have to take care of Brooklyn. He is my responsibility now and even with backup from my Pony Club manual and Google I know I can't do it all on my own. I don't know enough. I need help, but no one seems dependable.

Declan stands and appraises Brooklyn. I pray he doesn't say he's not a bad little fellow. I don't want Brooklyn busting the cross-ties and taking Declan by the arm. Or throat. He looks over at Kansas for a second, and I don't know if it's my blurry vision, but it seems to me that she quickly shakes her head then looks away. She's acting like there's some secret she doesn't want me to know.

Declan crosses his arms across his chest. His biceps bulge out below the short sleeves of his t-shirt. "Now this is a fine animal," he says.

Kansas drops the hose and water sprays into the air as the nozzle hits the cement. Kansas jumps but Brooklyn stands steady as a rock, his eyes fixed on Declan.

Declan steps forward and runs a hand along Brooklyn's spine, over his rump and all the way down the right hind leg to the fetlock which he grabs briefly before Brooklyn raises his foot. "Well now isn't this interesting," says Declan examining the hoof. He lowers it gently, inspects the other hind foot. Then he moves to Brooklyn's left shoulder, bends and squeezes the fetlock; Brooklyn shifts his weight to his right foot and lifts the left. Declan sweeps the sole with the palm of his hand, presses the sole with his thumbs then lowers the foot and turns to me. "Two things here about your pony. First, did you see how agreeable he was about picking up his left foot when he has pain in the right? Second, his feet are an unusual shape, and it's a sin how they've been neglected, but the walls are thick, the soles are solid and concave. We'll have him fixed in no time."

"I'm just glad he didn't bite you," I say.

"Bite me? Now why would he do a thing like that?" Declan pats down Brooklyn's mane and forelock which have been standing up like a Mohawk, and takes a quick look at Brooklyn's ears. With his mane lying down, the ears look even bigger. Could this be a trait of young unicorns before they turn white?

"He bit the transport driver when he called him *not a bad little guy,*" I say.

Kansas says, "I hardly think that was why—"

Declan ignores her. "Well can you blame him? *Not a bad little guy?*" He snorts with disgust. "Let me get my tools, we'll check out that right front."

While he's out of earshot digging around in the back of his truck, Kansas murmurs, "I've never heard him talk so much."

"You don't think he's just being nice, do you?" I say, but Declan returns before Kansas can answer.

He buckles on his leather farrier chaps, takes a short curved knife from his tool box and sets to trimming Brooklyn's foot.

I watch Kansas staring at Declan's backside. She hasn't stopped smiling since he got here. "I have another new boarder," she tells him. "He came in with this one, from the prairies."

Declan grunts.

"He's a beauty. Huge. 17.2 hands."

Declan shakes his head. "Horses weren't meant to be that big. Good luck keeping him sound. Horses are supposed to be this size." He gestures with an elbow towards Brooklyn's ribcage.

"Oh not this small," says Kansas.

"I know you women like them bigger, but if you left everything up to Mother Nature you'd never see a horse over fifteen hands. This may hurt a bit, son," he says to Brooklyn, "but if we can find the abscess and release it you'll be glad when we're done." In quick succession he flicks off several bits of sole with his knife.

"But you know, the conformation on the other one is fantastic," says Kansas. In my opinion it's rude to be talking like this in front of Brooklyn, and maybe if Kansas wasn't so set on impressing Declan she'd be thinking the same way. "He has a neck like a swan and the slope of his shoulder . . . ." Kansas stops momentarily when she hears Declan scoff, but then she starts up again. "He's a very well-bred animal. He's a branded Hanoverian. They've been breeding them selectively in Europe for decades."

Now she's really showing off. This is so disappointing. One of the things I like about Kansas is that she isn't a lecturing know-it-all, and here she is lecturing Declan of all people.

Declan lowers Brooklyn's hoof, slides the knife into the sheath stitched on his chaps. He stands and stretches his back, then strolls to Kansas's side. He doesn't look at her, but turns so they can both watch Brooklyn, then he leans against her shoulder. A red flush works its way up Kansas's neck and her smile disappears.

"And his feet?" says Declan. "What are they like? Can he go barefoot like this one or will we be looking at re-shoeing every five weeks to stop his walls from falling apart?

And some nutritional supplements as well, I expect. A load of biotin in his feed. Of course the feet may not be bad now, coming from the prairies, but a wet winter on the coast will tell a different tale."

"You haven't even seen him," says Kansas. Her cheeks are flaming red.

"Now this pony of Sylvia's is another matter," he says ignoring her completely. I wonder if he's really so dense that he doesn't know what's going on, and all he notices is the horses. "Once his feet are trimmed up properly, you'll see. Strong walls. Good angles. Straight legs, my god look at him, he could be right out of a textbook. And not a mark on those legs, no splints, no wind-puffs—for a middle-aged fellow, he's got the legs of a five-year-old."

"Middle-aged?" I say. "I thought he was young, because he was still grey and hadn't turned white yet. Kansas told me that's what happens with greys."

I look at Kansas to confirm this, but she's dabbling her boot in a puddle of water left on the floor and won't meet my eye.

"Well he's not exactly young," says Declan. "Not that it matters, because a pony that's built like this one has lots of miles left in him."

"How old?" I say.

"Didn't the vet tell you, from the pre-purchase exam?"

"What's a pre-purchase exam?" I ask.

Declan turns to Kansas and another of those annoying unspoken adult messages passes between them. Perhaps two messages, because Kansas breaks her gaze and studies the floor.

"Well then let's have a look at his teeth," says Declan and moves back to the pony.

My heart races. If Brooklyn maims Declan, Kansas will never ever forgive me.

But Brooklyn stands calmly as Declan strokes his face. Declan's fingers linger momentarily over the scab in the middle of his forehead, then slide down and part Brooklyn's lips to expose his teeth.

"Jesus Christ," says Declan. "Would you look at these fangs?"

My stomach turns over and I swallow hard to suppress a retch. A sharp-toothed unicorn is what frightened Taylor so badly. That was in my dream world, but there are so many cross-overs now between that world and this one my head is swimming, my vision is blurring. I blink hard three times, try to focus on something, and find Brooklyn's right front foot, though now there seem to be two of them.

"When's the last time this pony had his teeth floated?" says Declan. "You'll attend to that, will you Kansas? Have the vet out to do this?"

I warily swing my vision to Kansas who has told me before that she is a boss mare who doesn't like being told what to do, but a blurry Kansas is nodding agreeably, as though nothing would please her more than following instructions from Declan.

If this is what happens to people who are in love, I want no part of it.

"Now let me finish that foot," says Declan.

Brooklyn lifts his foot and Declan flicks away at it some more with his knife. A cloud of white shavings drifts down over the toe of Declan's boot. I watch for a moment, but everything is looking fuzzy so I close my eyes. I hear the snicking sounds of the knife, I feel a headache building, and wonder what will happen first. Will my head explode or will my entire stomach fling itself out of my mouth?

The cutting sounds cease abruptly and Declan says, "What's this now?"

My eyes pop open and I can just make out Declan using what looks like it might be a screw-driver to pry something out of Brooklyn's foot.

"You found the abscess?" says Kansas.

"Not an abscess." He holds an object between thumb and finger. "This was jammed in between the frog and the sole of his foot."

"A rock?" says Kansas, who doesn't have a good view.

"I don't think so," says Declan. He has lowered Brooklyn's foot and is using his knife to scrape at the thing. "I thought it might be a chunk of wood, but it's harder than that. Looks like a bit of bone. Or antler maybe."

I lean my back against the barn wall for support. My legs go wobbly and slowly I slide until I'm sitting on the cement floor. I know what the thing is. It's a piece of broken unicorn horn. Now everyone's going to know.

CHAPTER SIX

They don't know. Neither of them figures it out even though it's totally obvious. So I don't say anything.

I manage to eat some apple for lunch, but the headache gets worse. I almost tell Kansas about it, but then she says I still look pale and maybe I should go home and rest. Brooklyn can use some more time to settle in, she says. There's no hurry to be riding him and Kansas has to pick up hay this afternoon anyway. She won't have time to give me a lesson. I reluctantly go along with this. I don't have the strength to resist. I even let her throw my bike in the back of her truck and drive me home.

I let myself into the house with my key, pull the drapes in my bedroom and lie down for a nap. I hope I don't dream, I don't have the strength to deal with the unicorn right now. I wake up when I hear my mom's car clanking into the garage, followed by voices on the front walk. My head still aches. I don't want company, but I recognize the sounds of Auntie Sally, then Taylor. Slowly I lever myself off the bed. I open the drapes, blink hard to focus, hear Taylor tapping at my door and tell her to come in.

"You okay?" says Taylor.

"I just had a little nap."

"A nap? What are you—four?"

I'm surprised to hear Taylor sounding sarcastic like her older sister Stephanie. Perhaps sarcasm is something that occurs naturally in mid-adolescence. I'll know soon enough: as soon as I officially enter puberty my mother will provide all the information I never wanted to know about my next developmental stage. Maybe there will be scientific studies showing the link between estrogen and sarcasm. A shiver goes through me. Estrogen treatment is the next phase, once the growth hormone has done its job. Who knows what side-effects will come with that.

Taylor does one of her highland dancing stretches while surveying my room, or perhaps it's a ballet move. She's wearing shoes that look like ballet flats, little canvas things with thin soles. She lifts on and off the points of her toes and spies the horse stickers on my light switch. "Oh I like those—where'd you get them?"

"The Dollar Store," I say.

"Did you notice if they had any angel things?"

I try to remember. All I ever notice is horse things. "I guess."

"It's not far from here is it?"

"Five minutes on my bike."

"Double me," says Taylor.

"I'm not allowed to double," I say, much too weakly. I know how this is going to go. Taylor is a year older than me and difficult to resist at the best of times, and this is not the best of times. On the other hand, I still feel guilty about drawing Taylor into the dream with the unicorn so if I can help her redecorate her bedroom it will go a long way towards making amends.

"No one will know," says Taylor. "Our moms are having a glass of wine on the patio. We'll be back before they notice."

Taylor takes me by the arm and drags me out to the garage. This would be a good time, I think, to start acting like a boss mare. Kansas has told me all about herd dynamics. Hambone rules by being a bully; Kansas says the mares go along with him but deep down they resent it and eventually they'll make him pay. When Hambone is not out in the pasture, Electra is the boss mare, but she's subtle about it, so Photon wants to follow her around. I can't imagine Taylor wanting to follow me around. If I stand up to her, she'll escalate and treat me like a baby. Electra has more indirect methods for being a boss mare, but for the life of me I can't imagine subtlety diverting Taylor. She is clearly on a mission. She has already seated herself astride the carrier behind my bike seat. "Giddee-up!" she says.

It takes a while for me to get used to the extra weight on the back of my bike and then there's the backward pull from Taylor's hands on the top of my shoulders, but Taylor says she's ridden this way a million times with no problems. In my peripheral vision I can see Taylor's legs spread out to the sides, toes not pointed for a change, but turned up to stay off the road. The bike wobbles a few times, but despite my headache, I get the hang of it and by the time we reach the Dollar Store everything seems to be under pretty good control.

I lock up the bike and follow Taylor into the store. I tag along, feeling like a puppy. I'm not pleased with myself. It's difficult to be a boss mare. Even difficult for Kansas under certain circumstances it seems, and she's had years of experience. I wish I could figure out how Electra manages it. She bosses Photon who is bigger and older.

Taylor skims up one aisle and down another, finding angels everywhere. Certainly she has much more choice than I had when I was looking for equestrian-themed supplies. In the house wares section she finds an angel coffee mug, angel candlestick holders, angel salt and pepper shakers. In the stationery section there's a pack of dove grey computer paper with faint white feathers floating down the pages. I find a thin sleeve of angel stickers for her and at first Taylor says she's outgrown that sort of thing but then she looks at me in that kindly spiritual way that drives me crazy because it makes me feel like I'm three years old. "Okay, for you, I'll take them," and she adds them to her stack of stuff. There's a small clothing section in the back corner of the store. Taylor discovers a pink t-shirt with two white angels embossed on the front. There's also a rack of scarves. She rubs the fabric between thumb and finger. "Do you think this is silk?"

"Not at two for five dollars," I tell her. I would be more supportive if I was feeling better.

"I'm sure it's silk," says Taylor, flicking through the display. She pulls down a flimsy length of sky-blue covered with fluffy white clouds, and on each cloud is an angel playing a harp. "Can you believe this?" she says. "I can wrap it around my ecru lamp shade. It is so perfect!"

"Hay crew?" I say. She has reminded me that Kansas is stacking hay today, and she wouldn't let me help her because she thought I wasn't well enough and now here I am shopping with my cousin who, frankly, I can't imagine owning a lampshade decorated with people stacking bales of hay.

Taylor stares at me, blinking, then her eyebrows twitch up. "That's *ecru*, Farmgirl. It's a colour, kind of like eggshell if you really need the agricultural reference."

At the checkout she spies a tub of magic wands, hard plastic tubes filled with blue fluid and stars that flow back and forth when the wand is turned. "This is my lucky day!" says Taylor. "I've wanted one of these forever!" She places one firmly on top of her stack of merchandise. The cashier rings it up and stuffs everything into a large plastic bag.

"Didn't you bring a backpack?" I ask as we leave the store. "How are you going to carry all that?"

"Easy," says Taylor, slipping an arm through the handle holes. "Watch me."

Of course I can't watch—I have to keep my eye on the road. I take my seat on the bike and feel Taylor climb on behind me. Taylor's hands return to my shoulders and the shopping bag lies sandwiched between us. The magic wand sticks me in the armpit. Somehow we glide out of the parking lot onto the roadway.

"Where's that stable you go to anyway?" says Taylor. "Why don't we drop by and you can show me this new horse of yours?"

"It's too far," I say, pedaling as hard as I can up a hill. We must have coasted on the way to the store. I hadn't really noticed, because it was easy. In this direction it's up-hill and Taylor's hands tug at me. I can feel what must be the candlesticks digging into my spine.

"Go on, we can do it, I'll flap my angel wings!" says Taylor and one of Taylor's hands lets go and the plastic bag is pulled free. It crackles in the wind and the bike wobbles.

"Don't do that!" I tell her.

Taylor laughs and does it again and then puts her hand back on my shoulder and the bag returns against my back where it rustles every time Taylor shifts her weight.

"Take me or I'll use my magic wand to put a spell on you!" says Taylor, which is totally unfair. Taylor has frightened me before with her spiritual interests in palm-reading and Ouija boards. I want to go home, my head is pounding, it feels like someone is sticking a knife in my forehead. I want to lie down in the dark in my bedroom.

"I bet it's up this road. Turn here!" Taylor leans to the left. She's guessed correctly. Somehow she's picked the road where Kansas lives. I have to turn the bike if only to stay upright.

"Isn't this fun?" says Taylor.

Over the rustling sounds of the plastic bag I hear a vehicle approaching from behind. As it draws closer, it sounds more like a truck than a car. I hope it isn't Kansas. Kansas will kill me for riding my bike like this. I suddenly realize that Taylor isn't wearing a helmet and Kansas is fanatical about protective headgear. I guide the bike as close to the edge of the pavement as I dare. The vehicle slows behind us and the driver honks the horn.

"Pass, you idiot," says Taylor.

I feel Taylor's hand let go, and the pressure of the bag disappears. I turn my head marginally, to see Taylor's left arm extended, the bag hanging from it, as she indicates to the driver to go around. Except there are two bags, and two arms. I am seeing double again. I look ahead and feel a swell of nausea. The bike wobbles badly.

"Hey!" says Taylor. "Watch it!"

The front tire slips off the pavement into a rocky rut

beside the road. Taylor's hands clutch at me then her foot bangs against my calf and I push as hard as I can on the pedals, straining to keep the bike upright and moving ahead.

"Oh no," says Taylor, "my foot…" and then all I hear is her screaming.

CHAPTER SEVEN

I can't get up. I'm on my hands and knees and if I raise my head it pounds like crazy. I'm afraid to open my eyes in case everything is still double. I know my bike is beside me, and Taylor is close by because she's yelling and she's as loud as a trumpet in my ear. And then there's a hand on my back, and a familiar voice asking if I'm all right and did I hit my head. It's Kansas.

"I'm okay. I didn't hit my head," I say, though it feels like there's a spike going through it. I fumble with the buckle of my helmet until it releases, slides off and bounces on the pavement. "My cousin Taylor is hurt. I crashed the bike. It was my fault."

"It wasn't your fault. I was right behind you in my truck. Taylor was waving her arm around trying to get me to pass, but I couldn't, my truck is loaded with hay, there wasn't enough room. She threw you off balance, it wasn't your fault."

I hear another familiar voice trying to soothe Taylor.

"It's okay," says Kansas. "We're lucky, Kelly Cleveland was right behind me. She's helping Taylor now."

"But it was my fault," I say. "I let her boss me even though I had a headache and I was seeing double. From the growth hormone," I add emphatically.

I flop sideways so I'm sitting on the edge of the pavement. Warily I open my eyelids to a tiny slit, so I'm looking at the world through my eyelashes. The double vision has cleared, but I wish it hadn't. There's blood all over the place. Taylor is lying on the grass at the side of the road. Dr. Cleveland is easing the shoe off her foot. The cap is full of blood . . . and something else. I tell myself to stop watching, but it's too late. A toe slides out of the shoe, rolls across the pavement and onto the dirt at the side of the road. The toenail has pink polish on it, with sparkles.

Taylor has stopped screaming.

Kansas groans and leans close.

"She's a dancer," I say.

Kansas tells me to sit still and she'll be right back. She crouches at Dr. Cleveland's side. "Her name's Taylor," she tells Dr. Cleveland. "She's Sylvia's cousin. She's a dancer."

Dr. Cleveland fixes her with a brief sad look, then checks Taylor's pulse. "I think she fainted," she says. Gently she lays Taylor's arm back on her side. "Kansas, do you have anything we could use for a tourniquet?"

Kansas looks around and spies the shopping bag. She drags it out from under my bike and empties it on the pavement. Dr. Cleveland rifles through the pile, then knots the scarf around Taylor's ankle, forms a loop of fabric, inserts the blue wand with stars and uses it to wind the scarf tight.

"A magic wand," says Kansas, shaking her head.

I wish someone would use it to make the accident unhappen.

Dr. Cleveland nods. "Abracadabra," she says, using the free end of the scarf to tie the wand securely against Taylor's leg. Then she folds the t-shirt into a square not much bigger than her hand and presses it against the end of Taylor's foot. "Don't suppose you have a baggie," she says, indicating with a nod of her head towards the toe still lying in the dirt. Kansas says no. "Fine, we'll leave it for the ambulance guys," says Dr. Cleveland. "How's Sylvia?"

"She has a headache, and double vision," says Kansas. "She says she had it before the crash, she says she didn't hit her head. She was wearing her helmet."

Dr. Cleveland nods.

Kansas says, "Sylvia says it's from the growth hormone."

Dr. Cleveland stares over at me for a long moment as she thinks. "Oh Christ," she says finally. "I'll bet she has increased intracranial pressure. She needs to come off that stuff right away. It's a rare side effect, and would account for the headaches, nausea, vomiting. Someone should have picked that up." She stops abruptly. "I shouldn't have said that."

In the distance I hear the swells of a siren. Kansas comes back and sits beside me. She strokes my back and I start to cry.

"Don't worry," says Kansas.

"Is Taylor going to die?"

"No. She's hurt her foot, that's all."

The sirens are deafening. Car doors open and close, radios splutter. I shut my eyes tight. "I'll never make up for this if she has to take time off dancing," I say.

"Look," says Kansas, "Did you hear what Dr. Cleveland said? She says you're right about the growth hormone causing your headaches, and you'll have to come off the stuff. That's all it is, a side effect."

I snuffle. "So I'm going to stay short."

"Looks that way."

"But I've got my horse anyway."

"You've got your horse."

I hear steps in the gravel and open my eyes just enough to see an ambulance attendant kneel beside me. He reaches for my wrist and takes my pulse. "You have a horse?" he says.

"And he's a fine animal," says Kansas mimicking Declan but with a really terrible Irish accent.

"You really think so?" I say, more grateful for a lie than I ever have been in my life.

CHAPTER EIGHT

I'm dreaming. I'm with the unicorn, though without a horn I'm not sure if he is a unicorn anymore. He's joined the ranks of "the hornless ones", which used to be his dismissive term for horses. I haven't heard him say this for a while. If he wasn't always so grumpy I'd feel sorry for him.

"It's time for you to start building some bridges," says the unicorn.

"I thought I wasn't supposed to—I thought it was against the rules."

"You were warned not to build bridges until you had more control. Your control in this realm is acceptable now. Though the other realm remains problematic I'm sorry to say."

"So I can name people and bring them into my dreams if I want?"

"If you wish," says the unicorn.

"But I have to have better control in the other world?"

"I believe I said as much," says the unicorn unhelpfully. He can be so infuriating.

"I don't get it. I'm a kid. The adults are in charge. I don't have control of anything."

"Hmmph," says the unicorn. "If you drew more from

this realm when you were in the corporal realm you might fare better. Bridges have been known to operate in two directions." He uses his ironic tone, which brings out the worst in me.

"Are you on drugs?" I say. "Because you're making even less sense than usual."

"If you took some time to think about it instead of reacting immediately, you might have asked a more sensible useful question," says the unicorn.

I don't want to think about it. I don't want to think about anything, because there's something unpleasant at the back of my mind that I need to avoid. I prefer to change the subject. "You don't seem to be limping as much," I say.

"Thank you for noticing," says the unicorn. "I'm glad you're not totally wrapped up in your own problems for a change."

"My problems aren't exactly insignificant."

"Medication side effects may be unpleasant at the time, but seeing as how they will disappear when you do away with those awful injections, I don't see that you have much to complain about. Your headaches are hardly a permanent condition."

"You're sure?"

The unicorn snorts.

"But I'll be stuck with being short forever."

"We discussed that previously. That is hardly a problem in the grand scope of things. Perhaps this will allow you to follow your heart's desire and become a jockey and gallop round and round on a racetrack in front of screaming crowds of gambling addicts."

"That is not my heart's desire and you know better. Why would you even say such a thing?"

The unicorn stops walking, lowers his head and eats some grass. His forelock fluffs out over the place where his horn used to be so I can't get a good look at it. I want to be able to compare it to the scab in the middle of Brooklyn's forehead.

"I don't know why you have to be so grumpy all the time."

The unicorn lifts his head, chews and swallows. A bulge of food slides down his esophagus, exactly as it does with the horses.

"Grumpy?" says the unicorn. "I do wish you wouldn't use that word. Though of course that's what your parents say to you when they see you sad or angry. I find it exceedingly patronizing myself."

I sigh. "You're right. I'm sorry."

"There are better ways of finding out what's troubling somebody."

"Like what?"

"Well you could ask me."

I consider this. I think about all the times I've been upset and how nice it would have been if my parents had asked me what was the matter instead of pointing out that I was acting grumpy. "Okay," I say, "what's troubling you?"

"Nothing." The unicorn looks at me straight-faced, then bursts into laughter. His laugh is very strange, and it's exactly the same as the strangled bugling noise that Brooklyn made from the back of the transport trailer, though what he had to laugh about then I still can't figure.

"You're funny," I say, and I laugh too.

"Laughter is the best medicine," says the unicorn.

"Oh brother that's so corny," I say, but then I can't help myself and laugh some more. It makes me aware of the pressure of the pillow under my cheek, and I almost pop out of the dream except that the wind has caught the forelock of the unicorn to expose the scab and I'm drawn back in again.

I stare at his forehead. "What happened to you?"

The unicorn closes his eyes and drops his head. The only way he could make it more obvious that he was ashamed of himself would be if his cheeks turned flaming red, and maybe they are but under his white fur it's impossible for me to tell. When he starts talking he doesn't look at me but stares instead at a spot on the ground behind me. "I was bad. I strayed. I made a mistake and did something I wasn't supposed to do. It got smaller and smaller and I woke up one morning and it was gone—I was a flathead, just like when I was born."

I notice that he won't use the word *horn*. I reach over and stroke his cheek. Tears are welling behind my eyeballs. I feel the pressure along with the remains of a headache, but somehow manage to switch my attention back to the dream. I don't want to abandon the unicorn in such a state, and there's something about waking up that doesn't appeal either, something happened—something I don't want to think about.

"You mean unicorns are born without . . . I mean, they're born with flat heads?"

He huffs loudly. "Of course we're born with flat heads. Otherwise our mothers wouldn't survive the delivery. Our heads stay flat until puberty."

Automatically I tense as though I can expect a lecture on sexual development from the unicorn. Again I feel the pillow, and this time it's too much and I wake up thinking I've just missed a great opportunity to find out if unicorns are born grey and turn white like horses do, or whether some of them stay grey all their lives.

I don't open my eyes, but I know I'm not in my own bedroom. The smells are wrong and there's too much light and noise. And it all floods back to me, that I'm in the hospital. I keep my eyes shut as the memories unfold backwards in my head. How nice the nurses were last night when I couldn't sleep and one of them sponged my face with a warm cloth and held my hand and said I'd be fine. They just wanted to keep me in for observation overnight, and before that the ambulance ride, and before that . . . Taylor! Oh my god I'd forgotten about Taylor. They took her in a different ambulance. My eyes flicker open against my will, but I slam them shut immediately, because sitting on the end of the bed is my mom, and my dad is leaning on the door jamb sending a text message on his BlackBerry.

"Tony, do you have to?" says Mom. Her voice is deep and gravelly like she hasn't slept all night.

"I'm just telling them I'll be late coming in," says Dad.

"Late? You're going in to your office today?" says Mom.

Oh brother. You'd think that today of all days they wouldn't be at each other.

"I can't book off like you can, Ev."

"Of course you can. You could if you wanted to."

I think about opening my eyes and pretending I don't recognize them. That might change their priorities.

"We can't do anything anyway," says Dad. "She's in good hands here."

"Patients need an advocate," says Mom.

I remember her saying this all the time when Uncle Brian was in the hospital. My mom pretty well lived at the hospital when he was sick, and then he died anyway. This was before my mom went back to school and became a therapist, so she had more spare time.

"Well you can be the advocate, and I'll keep the home fires burning," says Dad.

"Oh right. . . ," says Mom with a sarcastic tone that I'm never allowed to use.

I've had enough. I open my eyes wide, smile at them and say hi.

"Oh thank god!" says Mom. She looks awful. There are bags under her eyes and she hasn't washed her hair. It's lying flat against her scalp and I can see her roots.

"Hey, Munchkin!" says Dad. He doesn't look much better, although at least his hair looks okay because its got so much natural curl it almost never looks bad. He sits on my bed on the other side from Mom and grabs my foot.

"How are you feeling?" says Mom. "How's your head? They say you have a concussion."

"How can I have a concussion? I didn't hit my head."

"You just don't remember hitting your head," says Dad.

"I . . . did . . . not . . . hit . . . my . . . head," I say very slowly and clearly so even they will understand. I remember telling the emergency room doctor the same thing.

"Uh huh," say Mom and Dad, exactly like the doctor said. No one believes me. I close my eyes in frustration and wipe my fingertips across my forehead . . . and feel a lump.

Could I have hit my head? I was wearing my helmet, which would have protected me. I try to remember what happened. I remember putting my arms out to break the fall, I remember rolling to the side the way that Kansas told me I should do if I ever come off a horse . . . and then I remember Taylor. I remember the blood all over the place.

I groan out loud. Big mistake.

"Do you have pain?" says Mom. "We'll get a nurse." She grabs the call button from beside my pillow and I grab it back from her quickly before she can press the button.

"No," I say, "I do not have pain, other than the stupid pain I get from the growth hormone. I was remembering Taylor, bleeding at the side of the road."

My mom takes my hand. "You have to focus on your own recovery, Honey," she says, but her eyes betray her for a fraction of a second and flick to the curtain separating my bed from the next one.

"Taylor, are you in there?" I call through the curtain.

Dad scoots up the bed then leans over and kisses me on the forehead. I flinch. How could I have hit my head and not remember? How could I have hurt myself if I was wearing an ASTM/SEI approved riding helmet like Kansas insists I wear all the time? The skin feels so tender. Dad doesn't notice. "She's not there right now, Munchkin, she'll be back later. She's down in surgery."

Mom shakes her head. "Tony," she whispers as though I'm not even there, "I told you we should have paid extra for a private room. This is going to be much too upsetting for Sylvie."

"Upsetting?" I say. "What's happened to her?"

Dad says, "It's a small thing. She injured her foot, that's all."

That's when I remember the toe and feel a surge of panic. "If she has to miss dance classes she'll never forgive me."

A dark look passes between my parents. My mom opens her mouth to speak but Dad reaches over and squeezes her shoulder and she presses her lips back together.

"What?" I say.

"We'll tell you later," says Mom.

"I hate it when you do this!" Maybe it's really really bad what's happened, maybe her whole foot had to be amputated after being damaged by my bike chain and she'll never walk again, maybe that's what they're protecting me from.

"We'll tell you when you're stronger, Snookie," says Dad. "Right now you need your strength to get better."

"Get better? There's nothing the matter with me! I'd be fine if I wasn't taking the stupid growth hormone! Ask Dr. Cleveland. Kansas told her all about my getting headaches and throwing up and double vision. I don't care if I'm short. I'm fine. What's happened to Taylor?"

My mom takes my hand. "Settle down, Honey. I know you're upset, but it's not appropriate to be demanding like this."

Dad says, "She lost her big toe."

"Thank Christ!" I say, and they look so shocked that I add, "Not her whole foot then?"

Mom shakes her head. "Language, Sylvie. Just the toe."

"So she could still dance," I insist.

"They don't think so," says Dad. "Apparently the big toe is very important for dancing."

I press deep into my pillows and close my eyes. "Poor

Taylor. That would be like me not being able to ride." I cover my face with my arm.

"She has to go off the growth hormone?" asks Dad. Now it's his turn to act as though I'm not there. "They told us there weren't any side effects."

"I'll look into it," says Mom. "I did bring the injector though, in case I needed to give her her medication."

"Don't you dare," I say.

"You don't mind if you stay short, Munchkin?" says Dad.

"What's so bad about being short, compared to being lame forever?" I sniff.

"Honey, don't talk through your arm," says Mom, "we can't hear you."

I flop my arm onto the bed and glare at my parents. I'm so ready to hate them, but then I see their concern and feel their pain on top of my pain and it's too much so I have to close my eyes again. I hate being a kid. This will be the worst part of staying short—people will continue to treat me as though I'm six. I have to find a way of dealing with this or I'll go out of my mind.

CHAPTER NINE

Kansas is sitting on my bed. Mom and Dad have gone home to "freshen up", but the way they were looking at each other I think they were ready for one of their "making up" sessions that happen after they've had an argument. Whatever. At least I won't be at home pretending I don't notice anything.

Kansas and I are whispering because Taylor is back from surgery and we don't want to wake her. She's hidden behind the curtain which is fine with me, I don't want to see her foot or what's left of it.

I can see that Kansas isn't comfortable in the hospital. Her shoulders are scrunched up around her ears and she jumps every time an announcement is made on the loud-speaker. Plus her eyes are shifty, which never ever happens at the barn.

I know she'll be more comfortable if she can talk about horses, so I ask her how Brooklyn is doing and she looks even more uneasy and she thinks a long time before she opens her mouth to say anything.

"I think he's very smart," she says, and when she sees my big smile she adds, "which isn't always a good thing."

"It's good in people," I say.

"It took me fifteen minutes to get a halter on him this morning," she says.

"What field was he in? Was he out with Electra?"

"He was in his stall."

I can't imagine Kansas chasing a horse around a box stall for fifteen minutes. She won't be feeling very good about herself. I don't know what to say.

"Then I lunged him," says Kansas. "I swear he was sound at the beginning but after two minutes he was so lame he was almost falling over. Then I put him back in his stall and run-out paddock and he was sound again."

"Oh no. I thought Declan fixed him." There is that small matter of the unicorn horn stuck in his foot that I don't want to talk about.

"That's what I thought. But we have to get the vet out to do his teeth anyway, so maybe she can have a thorough look at him. Probably he'll be fine. He's just got a bruised sole."

She doesn't sound convinced. I'm more and more sure she doesn't even like him.

I feel like I'm going to cry. Nothing is going right.

"And Taylor lost her toe," I say, sniffing. "She'll never dance again."

I reach for Kansas's hand. I've never held her hand before. It's rough and calloused and strong, not like my mom's or even my dad's hand but maybe like my grandpa's. For a second I think she's going to cry, too. She stares at me like I'm an orphaned kitten. "Oh, Sylvia," she says. "Everything will be okay. We'll sort it all out. The vet will help."

"My dad will hit the roof about the vet. He already thinks horses are too expensive."

Kansas nods. "Let's take it a stage at a time then.

She won't do an extensive workup without authorization anyway. I called her office. She could come tomorrow. Any chance you'll be out by then?"

I shrug.

A croaky voice emanates from the other side of the curtain, "You better not be out by then. You have to stay in here with me."

"Taylor!" I yell. I grab the rail of my bed, lean out as far as I can and whip back the curtain. It slides two feet and stops. Kansas has to get up and open it the rest of the way.

Taylor is lying flat out, her right leg propped on a pile of pillows. Fortunately her foot is so thickly wrapped with bandages that no one could tell there was a crucial piece missing. I wonder if Taylor remembers. A thin tube snakes from two bags on an IV pole and disappears under a patch of white tape on the back of her hand.

"Taylor, how are you feeling?" I say.

Taylor's eyes are half-closed. "I dunno. The drugs are good I think."

Kansas is looking wide-eyed at Taylor's foot, then mouths at me, "Does she know?" I give her a silent shrug.

Taylor peers in Kansas's direction. "Who are you?"

"I'm Kansas, Sylvia's riding . . . pal."

Taylor nods vaguely. "Oh yeah, I've heard all about you." Then she squints, trying to focus on Kansas's face. "Hey, weren't you there yesterday? On the road?"

Kansas nods.

"I thought so," says Taylor. She raises her leg, straight up from the mattress, with all the flexibility, strength and finesse of a dancer, and delicately repositions it on the pillows.

"Oh god," I moan.

"Good drugs, but my toe still feels very weird," says Taylor.

I lock eyes with Kansas in a panic.

Kansas says, "Maybe I should go."

She edges towards the door but stops dead in her tracks when I say quietly, "Don't you dare."

Kansas resumes her perch on the very edge of my bed, still ready to flee at the first opportunity.

I almost can't believe it. I've somehow done a boss mare trick, on Kansas of all people, and prevented her from leaving. Of course, I'm desperate because if Taylor doesn't know she's lost her toe, I don't want to be alone with her. I don't want to be the one to tell her, and I know I can't lie to Taylor. Sooner or later she will squeeze the truth out of me because Taylor is older and she's always done that. She's always been the one in charge.

Though who knows? With my new-found boss mare skills, perhaps I could even manage Taylor.

There's a light tapping sound at the doorway, and Dr. Cleveland's head appears around the edge. "Can I come in?" She says hi to Kansas then strides in between the two beds. "Sylvia, is it okay if I visit? Not everyone wants a psychiatrist in their room."

"We all know Sylvia sees a shrink," says Taylor. Her words are slightly slurred, almost as though she's drunk, and she's speaking loudly as though she doesn't care what anyone thinks.

"Hey, that's great. They put the both of you in one room," says Dr. Cleveland. "How're you doing, Taylor?"

"Oh fine." She sighs dramatically. "But my toe feels funny." Then she giggles. "Actually everything feels funny."

Fine, I think. A medical professional can handle this. Better still that it be a psychiatrist.

"That's understandable," says Dr. Cleveland.

"No pain though, because I'm on some really good drugs apparently." Taylor raises her hand with the IV needle then gently tucks it back at her side.

"Very good drugs, I imagine," says Dr. Cleveland.

I wish Dr. Cleveland would say something more instead of blandly going along with everything. Doesn't Taylor deserve to know the truth? This would be the perfect time to tell her because there are two adults present to deal with her fury and grief, and even more importantly, to protect me in case I get blamed for everything. I look to Kansas who is usually a confident straight-shooter type who tells things the way they are, but she is looking totally lost. I guess she isn't comfortable here in the hospital like she is back on her farm, in the barn, surrounded by thousand-pound animals. This is more Dr. Cleveland's territory, though of course Taylor isn't her patient. Not yet anyway. Probably later she will be, when Taylor loses her mind about losing her toe and her future with the National Ballet.

Maybe I should tell Taylor myself, and get it over with. It's not exactly fair because I'm the youngest, but perhaps this is part of being a boss mare. Electra for example is small and has to deal with Hambone all the time and how fair is that?

But then Taylor says, "I mean, I know it isn't there any more, but it still feels like it's there. It's as though part of my brain doesn't get it. And when I look at my foot, my toe still could be under all the bandages instead of lying in the dirt at the side of the road. It's very weird. Very very weird."

"Your brain will adjust," says Dr. Cleveland.

"But I like the drugs," says Taylor with a wobbly smile.

I can't think of what to say. I'm hugely relieved that I don't have to break the news to Taylor, but don't know how to approach the other matter.

"Though I suppose my dancing days are done," says Taylor with a small sniff. "And running, and basketball and volleyball—not that I liked any of those sports. I guess I'll be stuck on my butt for the rest of my life. Oh well."

Oh well? That's it? No drama, no *My life is over?* No *I will never forgive Sylvia for doing this to me?*

Dr. Cleveland says, "Well, Taylor, you've lost a toe, not a leg. There are lots of sports left for you to try. Hey, you could even join our riding club." She gestures to include me and Kansas.

This is a ridiculous idea. Taylor is afraid of horses. Taylor is actually afraid of a lot of things. Surely there will be an eruption.

"Right. Riding for the disabled. I've read about it," says Taylor mildly.

"You would hardly qualify," says Dr. Cleveland. "Not to mention that we're all disabled in some way. Right, Kansas?"

Kansas nods her agreement but I don't understand what they're getting at. I understand my own disability, my shortness, but can't imagine how Dr. Cleveland is disabled. She is perfect, and of course there's not a thing wrong with Kansas. Or at least I've never thought so, not on the farm where Kansas is in her element. I consider the ratty jean jacket that Kansas is wearing, her hair held back with the blue elastic from the bunch of broccoli. I like this look on the farm. Here it does look a little weird.

Dr. Cleveland says, "What do you think, Kansas, can people ride if they're missing a big toe?"

"Don't see why not," says Kansas. "All the weight-bearing is on the ball of the foot, though the idea is to get your weight into your heel, and on your thighs of course."

"Blah blah blah," says Taylor, her voice fading. I hope she is going to sleep, but then she says, "Hey. You're really a shrink?"

"Mmm hmm," says Dr. Cleveland.

"Well how come you're so tall?" Taylor giggles again. "Especially since you're— what, Chinese?"

She is so stoned. Though I've always wanted to know about Dr. Cleveland's background and never thought it appropriate to ask.

"My mother is Japanese-Canadian. My father is American-Basketballplayer," says Dr. Cleveland.

"That figures," says Taylor. She laughs, then falls silent.

"I think she's asleep," says Dr. Cleveland.

"I thought she'd be more upset," I say.

"It's difficult to be very upset about anything when you're on the right amount of morphine," says Dr. Cleveland. "How are you doing, Sylvia?"

"I'm fine. My head doesn't hurt so much. I want to go see Brooklyn."

"I've had a word with your pediatrician. He'll be in to see you later. I expect he'll be taking you off the growth hormone injections."

"And starting me on the estrogen treatment?"

Dr. Cleveland glances at Kansas, but her face remains unreadable. My mom says that all psychiatrists are like this. She insists it has nothing to do with being an inscrutable Asian, which would be racist. I find it unsettling anyway.

"I expect so, but probably not until you're out of hospital," says Dr. Cleveland.

Kansas punches me lightly on the thigh. "They're going to make a woman out of you one way or another."

I'm not sure how I feel about this, but I try to smile.

Kansas says, "Hey, Kelly, will they be giving her estrogen in that Premarin medication?"

Dr. Cleveland says, "I suppose so."

"You know what that's made out of, Sylvia? Pregnant mare urine. I know all about it because of the controversy about the PMU barns."

"What controversy?" I say.

"Oh the animal rights activists were concerned about the conditions these mares were kept in, and how some of the foals were sent to slaughter," says Kansas.

"I believe the industry has cleaned up its act," says Dr. Cleveland.

"Oh sure," says Kansas. "Only now the market is flooded with PMU foals which means regular back-yard breeders can't sell anything."

"Well, I...." says Dr. Cleveland.

"And there's another thing," Kansas interrupts. She may be out of her comfort zone here in the hospital, but the topic of conversation is home turf. Though it's odd because she's acting like a know-it-all and back home she never does this, except with Declan, who I guess also makes her nervous. "There's the problem of how badly socialized these foals are because they haven't been handled much by humans or properly raised by their mothers let alone spent any time in normal herds."

"I'm going to be taking mare pee?" I say. I don't care about the controversy, and I'm not even worried any more about whether or not I want to develop secondary sexual characteristics. What I'm contemplating instead is improving my chances of becoming a boss mare like Electra. "Can I start now?"

"Sylvia, you've got lots of time, there's no rush here," says Dr. Cleveland. She turns to Kansas. "So how's my boy settling in at the barn?"

CHAPTER TEN

Taylor stirs from the depths of her morphine-induced sleep. She calmly considers her bandage-swathed foot and sends a message to her absent toe to wiggle. The last time she saw her toe it was rolling across the pavement into the dirt at the side of the road. Perhaps it is still there, she thinks, though more likely a raven has flown by and eaten it. Oh well. She hopes the nail polish isn't toxic. She is vaguely surprised that she's not frantic, but it's so pleasant to be taking matters in stride, and really it's just a toe, there's more to life than this. Dancing will be a challenge, but she will deal with that. Or not. Whatever.

There is a hum of conversation from the next bed. She rolls her head to the side and attempts to focus. Closest to her is a very tall form—that must be Dr. Cleveland, still visiting. "I've had a word with your pediatrician . . . ." she is saying. Taylor closes her eyes, opens them, blinks rapidly several times. She loses track of the conversation. Her lids keep wanting to stick shut, but if she blinks and partially opens her eyes and looks through her lashes, something fun happens, she can see contours around people. Dr. Cleveland's lines are very straight and precise. They shimmer slightly whenever she talks. Sitting on the other side of Sylvia's bed is that odd person with the strange name. Taylor sends a leisurely probe back to an earlier conversation, though *how much earlier she couldn't say. Perhaps minutes, perhaps hours, well it doesn't matter. Slowly she extracts the name Kansas. She's never heard of anyone being named that before. It reminds her of the line from The Wizard of Oz: "We're not in Kansas anymore, Toto." Toe-toe, she thinks with amusement. And didn't Dorothy wear dancing shoes? Red shoes that she clicked together. Red toes. There had been a lot of blood. She won't want to wear sandals anymore, everyone will be staring at her toeless foot and feeling sorry for her. Kansas has fuzzy contours. She punches Sylvia's leg and a spark of light springs from the blankets. Sylvia's lines are a mess, broken and going off in all directions. And then everything changes. Kansas's lines firm up when she says words like <u>mare</u> or <u>foal</u> or <u>herd</u>. And Sylvia's contours fall into a more reasonable alignment and start leaping all over the place, she's excited about something. Then something really strange happens.*

"How's my boy settling in at the barn?" says Dr. Cleveland. Her lines soften and loosen and get pushed out by a kind of glow emanating from her dark skin.

"Oh he's a good boy," says Kansas and her lines soften too. "I watched him playing around in his paddock this morning. That boy can move."

Dr. Cleveland smiles and it's as though someone has opened the curtains and let in the sunshine. "And how's Brooklyn doing?" There's a clattering sound as she drops the guard rail then takes a seat beside Sylvia.

The light smudges around the three figures on the bed. It's very strange, thinks Taylor. She lolls her head off her pillow and back again so the contour lines and lights swirl into a kind of glowing soup.

"Kansas lunged him for me. He may not be sound. The vet's

going to look at him," says Sylvia. Taylor hears the concern in her voice but there is deep pleasure too.

"He probably just has a bruised sole," says Kansas.

Taylor thinks to herself, "Oh, a bruised soul, I can relate to that."

But then she's not quite sure if Kansas is telling the complete truth. She has a sense that Kansas is holding something back, but this doesn't seem to matter to anyone else. The three of them nod their heads and make humming noises of agreement and understanding. They look like a coven of witches. The light encircles them, emanates from them, encloses them, is thrown out from them, and stops short of Taylor, clearly excluding her. She closes her eyes. She doesn't like being excluded but she knows if she says anything to draw their attention the spell will be broken, and she'd rather be excluded than have that happen because there's something comforting and exciting about watching them. As though there was something that was possible about life that she didn't know about before. Not that it is totally unfamiliar, it's just that she wasn't really aware. There were times, in dance class, working in front of the mirror, watching herself and catching glimpses of the other girls . . . concentrating . . . stretching . . . listening to the music . . . moving as one . . . .

Her eyes close but she doesn't sleep this time.

"I can hardly wait to ride," says Dr. Cleveland.

"Me too," says Sylvia.

They sound exactly alike. They could be the same age, the same size.

"What level is Braveheart going?" says Kansas.

She sounds the same too.

Probably Dr. Cleveland says, "We were schooling third

level, showing second. But I'm so out of shape now, we'll have to go all the way back to training."

Probably Sylvia says, "Do you think that Brooklyn could do third level?"

"Well he's not exactly up-hill. So it wouldn't be easy for him, or for you. But we can try. If he's sound."

"I think he's sound. I think he's fine."

"A fine animal." Taylor thinks this is Kansas, but she's using an accent for some reason. Two people are laughing.

"What?" says the third person, who starts laughing anyway.

Taylor wants to laugh too. She wants to join them even though they speak a foreign language and she doesn't have a clue what they've been talking about. Something about horses. She recognizes that normally she's terrified of horses but right now she sees they're really nothing to be afraid of. They're just big animals. She hopes she can remember this. She wants to tell Sylvia that her thinking has changed, that she's not afraid any more. She strains at her eyelids to get them to open. They flutter, let in some light and she realizes that she prefers the darkness. Resting is good and she feels herself sliding back down towards that peaceful dark soft resting place. Oh well . . . .

CHAPTER ELEVEN

When I'm released from the hospital Mom picks me up and drives me home. She takes the day off work. I can't believe it. Mom never takes time off work.

She fluffs some cushions on the couch in the living room and tells me to lie down. She gets me a blanket. I'm still feeling kind of wobbly.

"Anything else you'd like?" she asks.

I think about asking for my Greenhawk Saddlery Supply catalogue, but it's hiding in my pile of comic books, and I'd rather she didn't know about it. "My Pony Club manual?" I say.

She looks a bit disappointed by this, but brings it to me anyway. Along with something else.

"I found these great visualization exercises," she says, leafing through a booklet. "They're wonderful for anxiety."

"Mom, I don't have anxiety. The headaches were from the growth hormone. Remember?"

"Honey, everyone can benefit from relaxation and visualization exercises."

Oh god. The hospital was better than this.

"Let me read you one," she says.

So I have to lie there, and close my eyes, and breathe

into my body, and go to my secret safe place, and then I stop listening. I fake it. I breathe slowly, and think about Brooklyn, and how it's going to feel to ride him, and whether he's going to be over his lameness, and whether things will be better at school in September if people know I own my own horse which makes me an athlete. Maybe Amber and Topaz won't care, they could tease me anyway and tell me I smell like a horse, as though that's an insult. But Logan Losino might be impressed. I wonder if he grew this summer. I wonder if we'll have any classes together this year, or maybe I'll only see him at lunch, and maybe not even then. Well, as long as I can ride every day, it won't matter. Or even if I can't actually ride, if I can just hang around the horses I'll be fine. I hope Brooklyn likes to be groomed. I imagine what it will feel like to lean against him and slide my fingers up his neck and under his mane . . .

Mom is saying that I need to come back to my body now and back to the room and, when I'm ready, to slowly open my eyes. I wait ten seconds, and open my eyes, and smile at her.

"Now, don't you feel better?" she says.

"Sure I do, you were right, Mom." And then I am struck by a brilliant idea, because if there's anyone who could use visualization exercises, it's my mom. "Now it's your turn," I say, reaching for her booklet. "Let me read one for you."

"Oh, no, Honey, I don't need that. You're the one in recovery."

"Mom, you said *everyone* could benefit. It's your turn."

She looks around as though there's nowhere to lie, so I toss one of my cushions on the carpet and point to it, and while she's getting settled I flip through the booklet looking for the best exercise for her.

I lead her through the relaxation part, where she has to breathe slowly and relax her toes and her fingers and everything in between.

"Now imagine you are going down an elevator," I read, "deep, deep into the Earth. It's lovely and dark and quiet and peaceful and you are completely safe, and totally in control of the elevator. You can put your hand on the control panel. There's a switch for the speed, so you can go faster or slower. There's a button to stop when you're ready, and another one to take you to the surface whenever you want so you're never trapped." This is pretty hokey, I think, but I glance at my mom and she has a very peaceful look on her face, so I keep going. "When you're ready, push the button to open the elevator door to your perfect secret safe place. Maybe it will be a cave or maybe it will be a meadow. Maybe you will be alone, or maybe there will be birds and animals and flowers, and maybe there will be a wise person. I'm going to be quiet now for five minutes, so you can explore your safe place. Perhaps you can ask someone a question while you're there, but I'll let you know when you have to come back." I lay the open book on my tummy and check my watch so I'll know when five minutes have passed.

I look at my mom. There are tears coming out of the corner of her eyes, but she looks really happy, and relaxed. I get a lump in my throat. I haven't seen her look like this for years. She even looks younger, but maybe that's because she's lying on her back and gravity is holding down her face so it doesn't fold forwards like it does when she's standing up and leaning over me like she does all the time because I'm so short.

When five minutes are up, I lift the book and start reading again. "Okay, it's time for you to leave your special place now. You can come back here whenever you want. Take your time. Make your way back to the elevator. Put you hand on the control panel. Close the door. Take a deep breath as you make your way to the surface. And another deep breath. When you get to the top, take a few seconds before you open the door."

I close the book. I wait for my mom to regain full consciousness. I don't think she faked it like I did. I think something really happened for her. Weird. I hear her adjust her head on the pillow.

"Oh Honey," she says. "That was wonderful. Thank you."

"What happened?" I ask. "Can you tell me?"

"Oh it was silly." She rolls to her side and slowly gets to her feet. "Something I haven't even thought about for a long long time. I'd forgotten actually." She looks at me, and her face is full of softness. "I'll tell you some time."

"Okay," I say, because it is okay. This is different from other times when she won't tell me things because she thinks I'm not ready. Now she's not ready. I can wait.

Then the phone rings. It's Dad. He wants to know if I'm okay. And my mom goes back to normal.

"She's fine, Tony, I'm helping her with some visualization exercises," she says. She taps her foot. "Well maybe you should try one yourself before you pass judgement." She looks over at me and rolls her eyes. "No, of course I'm not taking her out to see her horse. Do you want to talk to her?" I hold out my hand for the phone, but she shakes her head. "Oh, okay, we'll see you at dinner then." She hangs up. "He had another call," she tells me.

CHAPTER TWELVE

Kansas delays making the appointment with the veterinarian for two days until I'm back on my feet. She says it's a good idea for me to be there because Brooklyn is my horse and I'm responsible for him, as if I don't worry about that enough already. I wonder if the veterinarian can sue me if Brooklyn bites her arm off.

I'm still not feeling quite right, I guess from the accident or maybe I'm in withdrawal from coming off the growth hormone. So Kansas says she'll handle Brooklyn. She has him tied in his stall eating hay when my dad drops me off at the stable; she says she doesn't want to be chasing him around wasting the vet's time. We watch him over the stall door. I'm standing on a bucket, as usual. I didn't grow when I was in the hospital. This is going to be it for me, height-wise. A shrimp forever. I don't care.

"I'm making some progress," says Kansas. "It only took me ten minutes to get the halter on the little bastard this morning." Then she looks at me and apologizes.

"You hate my horse," I say.

"Oh no, Sylvia. Not at all. He's a challenge, that's all."

"You mean a challenge to your authority?"

"More like a training challenge. He'll be fine."

I think she's lying. I don't know what's worse, that Kansas thinks she has to lie to me or that she hates my horse. I stare at the stall floor. Already I'm feeling tired. Then I think: How would Electra handle this? And I fix Kansas in my sights.

"Kansas, if you don't hate him why did you call him a little bastard?"

Kansas has the decency to consider my question for a moment instead of reacting immediately like other adults do and tell me I'm wrong. She cranes her neck and studies the rafters above the stall. "Okay, Sylvia, you're right. I'm over-reacting. But I don't exactly hate him. I think I resent what he's done to your riding career. I wanted you to have the perfect first pony, and this guy's going to be tough. He's got some behavioural problems and some health and soundness issues. And his conformation isn't ideal, despite what Declan says."

I can tell by the end that she's softened a bit, but I don't know if it's just because she thought of Declan.

"Okay," I say.

Kansas clears her throat, but her next words come out sort of raspy anyway. "Sylvia, you're special to me. And I think you've got a great future ahead of you with riding. You have talent but more important you have heart. I'd hate to see that ruined by having the wrong first horse, and this can happen. It happened to my little sister."

I'm special to her? What does that mean? No one's ever said anything like this to me before. I don't have a clue how to handle a comment like this, so I say, "You have a sister?"

A truck honks in the parking lot, saving me from further embarrassment.

"The vet's here!" says Kansas quickly. I guess she's embarrassed too. "Let's get this show on the road."

Kansas pops into the stall, unties Brooklyn's rope and leads him out into the alleyway. I follow behind them. Kansas reminds me to stay well back, but I know all about that. I know how horses can kick. I see Brooklyn's muzzle touch Kansas's sleeve and his lips open a fraction. Kansas gives the rope a tug and growls, "Don't you dare." His great ears perk forward and he follows her mildly out into the sunlight.

When Kansas stops, Brooklyn halts squarely beside her just like a well-behaved well-trained horse would. His head turns and he looks at me, but then his attention is taken by the veterinarian who has climbed out of her truck and is walking towards us. Brooklyn's neck arches and a funny noise comes from his throat, almost like a whimper. I've never heard a horse make a noise like this before and I guess Kansas hasn't either because she looks at him in total amazement.

The veterinarian introduces herself to me. Her name is Dr. Bashkir but she says I can call her Tanya. I think she's really nice. She's probably a bit older than Kansas, and she's really pretty. Her hair is short, tidy and blonde with gold highlights. She apologizes for arriving late but says she had to attend a foaling emergency. Kansas has met her once before, back in the Spring when the horses were vaccinated and their teeth were checked for uneven wear. Kansas has told me she thinks Tanya is a great vet. She says Tanya's very smart.

"So what have we got here?" says Tanya, standing back and having a good look at Brooklyn.

Kansas says, "We don't know much. He was shipped

out from Saskatchewan last week. His previous owner broke his hip and ended up in extended care. He's an old friend of Sylvia's grandfather who bought the pony and sent him as a present. There are no registration papers."

"Well that doesn't surprise me," says Tanya.

Kansas looks at me for a second then carries on. "The pony was off on the right fore initially, but Declan, my . . . uh . . . farrier trimmed him up and carved out something that was pressing between his frog and the bar of the foot. I guess the pony could still have a bruise in there, but he seems fine in his paddock and hoof-abscess-lame when I lunge him in the ring."

"Oh," says Tanya. "Declan. I've met him."

I think Kansas was about to say something more about Brooklyn, but instead she slams her mouth shut.

Tanya takes a step toward Brooklyn, and I have to tell her to wait because Kansas hasn't provided some crucial information about Brooklyn, who is, after all, my responsibility. "You need to know his teeth are kind of sharp. And he bit the driver of the transport truck."

Tanya nods. "Thanks for telling me."

"Though he only bit him because the driver said Brooklyn was a not a bad little guy," I continue.

Kansas clears her throat but doesn't say anything. She's watching Tanya but doesn't look very happy with her any more. "How do you know Declan?" she asks.

I guess Tanya doesn't hear her, because she doesn't answer. She's focused on approaching Brooklyn. She lets him sniff her sleeve. "I suppose you've run into people who smell like me before," she tells him. She strokes his neck, runs a hand down his face then parts his lips to reveal his teeth. "Though it looks like it's been a while," she says. She wipes her hands on her pants. "I'll be wanting to tranq him, then use the power float on those teeth. I think we should test his soundness first before we load him up with drugs."

"My dad would say no x-rays," I say.

"There are money issues," explains Kansas.

"I understand," says Tanya. "Why don't we give him a good old-fashioned look-over?" She moves to stroke Brooklyn's forehead but her hand stops in mid-air. "Maybe we should have a look at this first," she says, gently lifting his forelock.

"I figure he scraped himself in the trailer," says Kansas.

"I don't think so." I'm horrified to see Tanya extract a pair of reading glasses from her chest pocket and perch them on her nose. "I think I may take a scraping here," she says uncertainly, taking a closer look. "Or maybe a biopsy."

"I don't think I can afford those," I say, hoping I can put off an investigation on money grounds. Some things are better left unknown. Such as whether or not unicorns really exist.

"Oh don't worry about it," says Tanya. "This one will be on me, to satisfy my professional curiosity."

"Brooklyn won't like it," I persist.

"Sylvia, it's okay, it won't hurt," says Kansas. "Or not much anyway, right Tanya?"

But Tanya is snapping into her latex surgical gloves, paying no attention.

Kansas tightens her grip on Brooklyn's halter and says to him, "We don't want you taking a piece out of the vet while she takes a piece out of you, now do we?"

But Brooklyn offers no resistance. In fact he acts resigned, if not depressed. Just like I feel.

Tanya quickly collects and bags her samples, then asks to examine the foot that Declan worked on.

"You don't have to hold him quite so short," she tells Kansas, indicating her death-grip at the top of the lead rope. "His head needs to be free if he's going to show us when he feels some pain."

Tanya picks up Brooklyn's foot. "Well, isn't this interesting," she says, just like Declan did. Then she pops his leg between her thighs and holds it there. She uses her hoof-testers to apply pressure to several points on Brooklyn's foot. Brooklyn doesn't flinch, but cranes his neck around and sniffs her bum. Kansas slides her hand back up the lead rope. Neither of us relaxes until Tanya lowers the hoof and steps away.

"Okay, Kansas, how about you walk him up the driveway and back and we'll watch how he goes."

As Kansas walks Brooklyn away from us, Tanya explains to me that she's watching for any irregularity in stride. I stand quietly so I don't interfere with her concentration. Kansas walks Brooklyn directly back to us.

"That looked fine," says Tanya. "Now again at the trot."

Kansas trots the pony away, stops, turns, and trots him back.

"Listen to the footfalls," Tanya tells me. After a minute she nods and says, "Regular as a metronome. And see that— no head-bobbing either." Then she calls out to Kansas, "And again, but I'll look from the side." And she repositions herself for a different view from the driveway.

Kansas is puffing by the time she's finished. Brooklyn looks like he's enjoying himself, as though he likes being the center of attention.

Tanya says, "Well he looks fine. You say he was unsound on the lunge? Why don't we try that before we get into flexion tests."

I grab the lunge line and whip from the tack room and we head over to the riding ring. Kansas leads Brooklyn in and shuts the gate behind her. Tanya leans on the fence. I climb up and stand on the bottom rail and hook my elbows over the top. This is kind of fun. I'm beginning to relax and enjoy myself. Hanging out with horses and horse women— what could be better?

Kansas moves to the center of the ring and sends Brooklyn out on a circle. He saunters along lazily until Kansas brandishes the whip and asks him to move forward with more energy. He staggers. I think my heart is going to stop. Brooklyn takes another step and nearly trips and falls.

"Yikes," says Tanya. "That's some kind of lame. Try him the other direction."

"Isn't that enough?" I say.

But Kansas turns him and asks for a walk in the other direction. Brooklyn doesn't have to be pushed this time before starting to limp. In fact he lurches more dramatically with each stride.

I groan. "Oh poor Brooklyn!"

Tanya puts her arm over her mouth and coughs. "Do you think you could get him to trot?"

"Really?" says Kansas. "The poor guy can barely walk."

"I don't want him to trot," I insist.

"I want to see what he'll do," says Tanya. "Just for a few strides. I don't think he'll come to any harm."

Kansas flicks the lunge whip behind Brooklyn and tells

him to trot. He pushes himself off his left front, drags the right, comes back down on the left and almost collapses.

"Oh no," I say. I think I'm going to cry.

Kansas looks at me and grimaces. "Sylvia, I'm sorry. But he'll be okay. Maybe it's the footing in here. Maybe it's too deep and it pushes on something in his hoof."

"There's nothing wrong with your footing," says Tanya. She coughs again, but there's a catch in the sound and I realize suddenly that she's trying not to laugh.

Kansas has noticed the same thing. She glares at Tanya. "You're laughing at some poor kid's lame pony?"

Tanya shakes her head. There are tears in her eyes. "Oh forgive me, but he reminds me of someone, a horse I had when I was young. He was my first horse too," she says to me, and then she laughs until the tears overflow.

My eyes might be about to overflow too, but not with tears of laughter. I am totally confused.

"Sorry," says Tanya. She takes a deep breath. "Let's try something. Would you be okay, Kansas, if he was at liberty in your ring?"

Kansas hesitates. "He's not easy to catch," she says. But then she shrugs and says okay. She unbuckles the halter, carries the gear back to the gate and slips through.

Tanya takes the lunge whip, moves away from the fence and flicks the whip into the yard. It cracks like a pistol shot. Brooklyn's head comes up and his ears perk but he doesn't move his feet. Tanya cracks the whip again and Brooklyn stares at her.

"I see," says Tanya. She turns to Kansas. "How about you go get that pretty little mare of yours and bring her into the yard for a visit?"

"Electra?" says Kansas.

"Right, the chestnut," says Tanya.

Kansas glances in my direction. "Electra won't want to visit," she says, then looks at me apologetically. "Electra doesn't like Brooklyn. Nobody does."

This is news to me, and I'm upset that Kansas hasn't told me, but more upset for Brooklyn. I know what it's like not to be accepted by the herd because that's what happens to me at school.

Tanya says, "Well, I'm not surprised, but go get her anyway."

Dr. Cleveland has told me that I'm teased at school because the kids notice that there's something unusual about me—my height, my fingernails, my ears. But I can't see what's so unusual about Brooklyn that would make the other horses not like him. Then I remember Tootsie, the hermaphrodite pony in England. Tootsie looked normal on the surface, but the other horses wouldn't accept him/her. They knew that underneath, things weren't right. I suppose it's too much to hope that Brooklyn is a hermaphrodite. At least hermaphrodites can be fixed with surgery, unlike unicorns.

Kansas takes the halter to the pasture. Hambone, Photon and Electra have heard the whip cracks and are watching her with interest. She collects Electra and brings her back to the ring. Electra balks when she spots Brooklyn loose in the ring. He whinnies at her, a high-pitched asthmatic bugling sound. Electra looks to Kansas as if to say, *Is he kidding? What kind of a whinny is that?* Kansas shakes her head. "Takes all kinds I guess," she says.

Tanya has been checking text messages on her phone

while Kansas was gone, which is fine because I'm too angry with her to make conversation.

"What now?" says Kansas.

Tanya says, "Lead Electra up the outside to the far end of the arena. Get her as close to the fence as you can."

Kansas does as she's told. When Brooklyn sees Electra at the end of the arena he puffs up and trots towards her.

"You can let them sniff noses, but just for a second," shouts Tanya. "Then bring Electra down to the other end."

Electra is reluctant, but eventually moves close enough to Brooklyn to touch noses. Their necks arch. Electra squeals. Brooklyn screams and strikes. Kansas leads Electra away and trots down the long side. Brooklyn trots along beside them inside the fence. In comparison to Electra, his stride is kind of short and choppy.

Tanya is killing herself laughing.

Suddenly it's obvious to me. "He's not limping," I say. "He was pretending."

"Ponies like this are one in a million," says Tanya wiping tears from her face.

Kansas is glowering at us. I expect she thinks there's some sort of conspiracy afoot: first Declan, now Tanya. I don't mind though. One in a million sounds pretty good to me. I'm actually feeling happier about Brooklyn than I've felt since he arrived.

And then Tanya says, "But there's something else you should know about him."

My heart sinks.

Tanya says, "I don't think he's pure horse."

Oh no. The examination of his forehead. She knows he's a unicorn.

"I think he's a hybrid," says Tanya.

Or part unicorn? This is a nightmare. I know what's coming, but as if there's some point in delaying things, like a complete idiot I say, "You mean like Dr. Cleveland's SUV?"

Tanya looks puzzled for a moment, but then she gets it. "Interesting," she says with a smile. "But not that kind of hybrid. I think he's a hinny."

"I knew it," says Kansas, then she looks at me sadly and says, "Well, I was pretty sure. But I didn't know how to tell you."

I don't know what a hinny is. I've never heard the word before, despite my basically memorizing the Pony Club manual and doing all my research on Wikipedia. But I'm afraid to ask, in case a hinny is a cross between a horse and a wayward unicorn.

I feel my life dissolving in front of me into something strange and inconceivable.

CHAPTER THIRTEEN

I'm sitting at the dinner table still kind of stunned and unsure how much to talk about recent developments.

Mom and Dad have been exchanging stories about their days at the office. Mom saw five clients and she thinks her practice is picking up. Dad saw six clients but talked to twenty more on the phone. He says he'd love to be back in those early days before his client load built up and he didn't have to work flat-out all the time. Maybe it's time he hired an assistant. That's when Mom asks me how my day went.

"Well, the vet came out," I say, hoping to lead up gradually to the more startling news about Brooklyn being a hybrid but apparently this was the wrong starter because Dad's fork drops on his plate with a clatter.

"The vet? Already we have vet bills? The horse just got here."

"Dad, I told you. He needed his teeth done. And his vaccines." I decide not to say anything about the biopsies since Tanya won't be charging for them. Or the fact that he's not exactly a horse.

Mom reaches over and pats my hand. "I remember, Honey. What was that like?"

Dad grabs a slice of bread from the plate in the middle of the table and asks for the butter dish.

"The dental work was really gross," I say. "The vet gave him a shot of tranquillizer then used something like one of Dad's power drills with a really long attachment and she ground off all the points and sharp edges from his teeth. There was smoke coming out of his mouth." Kind of like the smoke coming out of my dad's ears right now, I think, but I don't say that of course.

"I'll bet Brooklyn didn't like that, Honey," says Mom. "I hope you were well out of the way."

"Mom, he was tranquillized. He could barely stand up. And they had this metal thing holding his mouth open so he couldn't . . . ." I stop myself before I say "bite" because I don't want to remind them about what Brooklyn did to the driver. I want to keep my parents' opinion more on the positive side of the whole equation. "So he couldn't close his mouth. But this was after Kansas lunged him," I carry on quickly, having skirted dangerous ground. "She lunged him when I was in the hospital and she thought he was lame."

Dad has been spreading butter on his bread and the knife breaks through and scrapes his plate. "Lame?" he says.

"Oh Honey," says Mom.

"But he wasn't lame. He was pretending. Dr.Bashkir thinks he's one in a million." I'm almost there, I'm almost telling them, but then Dad says, "And what does your friend Kansas think?" His tone is ironic, probably because he thinks Kansas is a know-it-all since she has challenged his opinion on a few riding-related matters, like how my riding helmet is not "still perfectly good" since the accident and I have to buy a new one before I can ride again. Plus she put that hand-print on his shirt. Maybe he's still mad at her about that.

I am totally aware how fragile my new life with my own pony is. If the situation becomes too expensive, too risky, too anxiety-provoking, too anything, I'll be back to lesson horses and dreaming of one day owning my own, perhaps when I'm an adult with a job of my own, something that leaves me with lots of money and time for riding. Like when I'm forty maybe, and too old and stiff to ride. I guess I've made some progress from a few days ago when all I wanted was for Brooklyn to go back where he came from. "Oh, Kansas thinks he's great," I say.

Mom frowns, puzzled. "I thought you said Kansas wanted you to get an honest horse, especially for your first one."

"Well yeah," I say, "but just because Brooklyn pretends to be lame doesn't mean he's dishonest. I don't think." Really, I'm not sure.

"What the hell is an honest horse?" says Dad. "You ever see a picture of a horse brain? It's about the size of a walnut."

"Dad, it is not."

"Hardly big enough to think up ways of being deceptive," says Dad.

"Tony, I didn't know you'd studied comparative brain morphology," says Mom.

"I'm speaking metaphorically," says Dad. "You two are always anthropomorphizing."

"We are not," say Mom and I at the same time.

"Just a minute," says Dad raising his hand. His other hand dives in his pants pocket and comes out with his BlackBerry.

"Tony, not at the dinner table."

"I'd turned the ringer off, it was on vibrate. It's okay.

This is important," he says reading the display. He pushes his chair away from the table and heads to the family room. "Hey, Phil, did you get that FAX?"

Mom has that look on her face that means she's either going to cry or blow up like a volcano.

I hold out my empty plate to her. "Can I have more casserole please, Mom? It's delicious."

She serves a small spoonful. "I'm saving the rest for tomorrow," she says.

"Declan really likes Brooklyn too," I say, needing to talk about something, anything, even Kansas's private life if necessary. Talk of boys always grabs Mom's attention. She's ever-hopeful that I am taking an interest.

"And who is Declan?"

"He's the farrier. I think Kansas likes him. Her voice goes deep and mushy any time she talks to him or about him, and he's the only person that can tell her what to do."

Mom sighs. "Well. Your time will come too, Honey."

"I don't think so, Mom."

"You might be surprised what happens when you start the hormone treatments."

This reminds me of the Premarin. I put down my fork. "Mom, I've been thinking about that. I'm wondering if I could start right away."

The initial look of surprise on Mom's face is quickly passed by one of pleasure. She is so excited at my request that it's all I can do not to change my mind. I have to force myself to keep smiling. She leans forward and rubs the back of my hand. "Eager to get into adolescence?" she says.

I swallow hard and nod, though of course it's not true. From all I hear and see, adolescence is nothing to look forward to and, in an ideal universe, it would be outlawed. If my cousins are anything to go by, adolescence is nothing less than a long period of temporary insanity. I'm not interested in the estrogen. All I want is to ingest enough mare urine to feel like a boss mare like Electra.

"We'll have to check with the pediatrician of course. But won't it be exciting to have secondary sexual characteristics at last!" She is glowing, almost like Dr. Cleveland when she saw Braveheart coming down the ramp from the transport truck.

"That'll be great!" I say, but I can see my mom drawing breath and I know she's about to launch into one of her favourite educational talks about the joys of human sexual development. I quickly throw another subject-change at her. "Mom, have you heard how Taylor is doing? Is she out of hospital?"

"I don't know—I was at work all day. You could phone her later. Now Sweetie, I wonder if you remember what I told you before about what you can expect when—"

"Can I phone her now, Mom? It's a good time, because she won't have gone back to sleep yet."

Mom casts a disapproving look into the family room and sighs. "Why not?" she says.

I take the cordless phone into my room and close the door, partly because I want privacy but also so I don't have to listen to the argument when my dad comes back to the table.

Taylor is at home in bed, still groggy but now from Tylenol 3's.

"I can see why people become drug addicts," she says.

"Really?" I say. "I feel so much better now I'm not

taking that stupid growth hormone. I don't like drugs. Though I'm going to start taking Premarin soon I hope."

"I just can't worry about anything when I'm on this stuff," says Taylor, apparently not hearing whatever I have to say. "I'm not even worried about dancing. Isn't that weird? Though Stephanie says to not give up on the idea, she thinks I could still have a career as a lap-dancer."

"That's disgusting," I say. Though I'm not surprised. Taylor's older sister is always coming up with shocking ideas.

"Yeah, probably. But even Stephanie can't upset me right now. Do you think I'm a junkie?"

"No way."

"One thing I do worry about is what my boyfriend will say about dating an amputee."

"You have a boyfriend?" Taylor has never mentioned a boyfriend before. Of course why should she? She is a year older than me and therefore my opinion matters about as much as a flea's. Likely she wouldn't be saying anything to me now if the medication wasn't loosening her lips.

"Of course I have a boyfriend. He's away for the summer. His name is Franko. Franko Losino. Isn't that just the most perfect name?"

Losino? Before I can stop myself I find myself asking, "Does he have a younger brother named Logan?"

"Franko mentioned he has a bratty little brother." She pauses for a long time as the information slowly seeps into her drugged brain. "Oh Sylvia! Do you like him?"

I don't know how to answer this question. Sure I like Logan well enough, but not in the way that Taylor is implying. Last year he gave me a piece of gum, and he always seemed to be there at just the right time to distract

Amber and Topaz and keep their band of loyal followers from tormenting me. I've had two months of freedom from thinking about my life at school, and I'd rather not be thinking about it now.

Taylor misinterprets the silence. "Ooooh," she says, "Sylvia has a boyfriend!"

"I do not. No way. I have a horse. Well, not exactly a horse . . . "

"Maybe when you start taking estrogen you'll be more interested in boys. Maybe you'll want to trade in the horse and find yourself a really good boyfriend." Taylor giggles. I don't think she's making much sense. Taylor is sounding even sillier than she does when she talks about angels and spirituality.

"Why would I want to trade in the horse?"

"I'll tell you something very private," says Taylor. "Thinking about boys is even better than thinking about dance. So why wouldn't it be better than thinking about horses and riding?"

"Oh I don't think— "

"Don't you ever think about boys? I mean, I know your ovaries are wrecked from that Turner Syndrome, but don't you think about how great it would be to have a boyfriend, to have someone who loves you more than anybody else? Someone to hold your hand, to kiss you, don't you ever think about that stuff? I know I did when I was fourteen."

I look around my room at the horse posters, the horse figurines, the horse books, my scuffed riding helmet that I haven't replaced yet, my freshly polished Ariat Junior Performer paddock boots. "Oh sure," I lie. "All the time. I just didn't want to say in case my mom found out. You know how keen she is for me to enter my next developmental phase."

"I knew it," says Taylor. "Stephanie says you're a eunuch but I knew you weren't."

A *yoonick?* What is a *yoonick?* Or have I got the spelling wrong again? Maybe it's *unic?* Could a unic be half a unicorn? I'm not going to ask Taylor, not now when she's treating me almost like an equal. This is not a good time to let her think that I'm a moron, better for her to think I'm stupidly obsessed with boys, even if I'm not. I'm obsessed with horses. And I like being a horse-nut because that puts me in good company with Kansas and Dr. Cleveland.

"Logan Losino is so cute," I say.

And Taylor hangs up before I can tell her about Brooklyn being a hinny.

Mom and Dad are in the kitchen with the door closed when I get off the phone. They're having one of their intense discussions which always take a long time and then when they're done they usually go to their bedroom. So I know I have lots of time to myself on the computer in the family room.

I Google *hinny.*

Just like Tanya told me, hinnies are hybrids. They are a cross between a female donkey and a male horse. There's lots of really interesting information on Wikipedia, though more about mules which are hybrids of a female horse and a male donkey. Mules are more common because female horses and male donkeys aren't so fussy about who they mate with, including other species. Female donkeys and male horses are more particular. I like the idea that Brooklyn's parents were choosy about who they mated with. I think it's important to have high standards.

I find some sites that are full of technical information, including facts that Tanya didn't tell me about, but she'd only ever seen one hinny before in her life so she couldn't tell me as much as I needed to know. Or maybe I didn't hear everything she had to say because I was so relieved to hear that hinnies were a horse/donkey hybrid and not a horse/unicorn hybrid.

We'd studied genetics at school of course, but I can tell from my reading that as usual the teachers have left out some important facts. For example, no one ever told us that it made a difference which parent contributed what chromosome. Mules tend to look more like donkeys because coat colour and texture are passed on by the male donkey. In hinnies, the male horse provides the coat and also the gait, which explains why hinnies appear and move more like horses—except for the ears, which tend to be long-ish, like Brooklyn's, though not as long as a donkey's fortunately.

Behind me I hear the kitchen door creak open, then my parents whispering as they sneak down to their bedroom. Mom giggles. Their door shuts tight and I am spared hearing any more. I'm glad they've made up already, but still.

Fortunately I am really enjoying myself. I like learning. I like understanding more about Brooklyn. I like being the only person around who owns a hinny. I like it that hinnies have the high intelligence of the donkey and the amenability of a horse. They sound so perfect, and I am so lucky. When I grow up I think I will become a veterinarian who specializes in hinnies.

I feel all relaxed and happy so I scroll back up to some technical stuff about chromosomes that I skimmed over the first time.

I swear that my heart stops.

Because there, right on the screen, is information that totally changes my life.

Hinnies are missing a chromosome.

Just like me.

Hinnies are sterile.

Just like me.

There's nothing wrong with hinnies. No one talks about "hinny syndrome". Hinnies are perfectly normal and natural.

And maybe the same thing applies to me. Why not? Maybe there's nothing wrong with me and I don't have Turner Syndrome.

I am a hybrid. I know it in my bones.

But a hybrid of what?

And I remember that Stephanie said she thought I was a unic. Half a unicorn.

I rub my forehead.

There's that bump under my skin that I noticed in the hospital. I'm sure it's bigger now. It's kind of sore. The more I rub it the more sore it gets.

CHAPTER FOURTEEN

I am riding, and not on Electra so immediately I suspect I'm dreaming. Sometimes when I ride Electra in a lesson I feel like maybe I'm dreaming, but mostly I notice that I'm working hard and concentrating on what Kansas says about things like my weight being equally distributed on my feet, thighs and seat bones and my shoulders being square, so I don't have time to think about whether it's real or not.

I'm riding a white horse, so possibly I'm riding Kansas's horse Photon. Then the head turns, and I see I'm riding the grumpy unicorn, though his horn is still missing.

"I thought you didn't want me riding you? You said it would be undignified," I say.

"Well it is. But sometimes we have to put up with life not going the way we want it to."

He plods on. He's not limping but he's not very energetic, not like the galloping and jumping dreams I usually have. There's something I need to ask him, but I can't think what it is.

The unicorn says, "And don't kick me, or try any of that giddy-up nonsense."

"Okay," I say. I can feel his warmth underneath me and the gentle swaying of his movement. Brooklyn probably wouldn't feel this good, not with his spine sticking up and his ribs poking out.

Then I remember. "There's nothing wrong with me. I'm a hybrid," I tell the unicorn. This was part of it anyway. There's something else though. My brain feels fuzzy.

"So you won't have to go on that Premarin stuff," says the unicorn.

"Of course I do. I still want to become a boss mare."

He snorts. "That will take more than mare pee."

"I know that," I say. I try not to sound defensive. And I do know. I just don't know exactly what more I'll need.

"And of course there will be the side effects."

"Not everyone experiences side effects from medications. And not all side effects are bad. I know someone," I say, pleased with myself for not mentioning Taylor's name, "who got pretty blissed-out on morphine and Tylenol 3."

"And you'll grow hair," says the unicorn.

"I'll shave it off, like my mom does." She has a pink razor she keeps by the bath tub. I could buy my own, but not pink.

"Well don't you think that's stupid?" says the unicorn. "You want secondary sexual characteristics and then you shave them off?"

This unicorn is like Stephanie on a very bad day.

"And your sweat will smell," he continues. "You'll get acne. And your mammary glands will develop."

"I'm going to wake myself up," I threaten.

"About time too."

"You don't want me to grow up. You want me to stay a little kid. You're just like my dad. My mom wants me to go galloping off through the developmental stages and become a full-blown woman as soon as possible, but you and Dad want me to stay as your little girl."

"Now you're cooking," says the unicorn.

ᔭᐟ

As soon as I wake up I remember the crucial matter I failed to discuss with the unicorn. I meant to ask exactly what sort of hybrid I was. I'm also puzzling over the roadblocks I keep encountering trying to grow up the way I want to . . . if I want to. I'm not sure I haven't thought of these issues before, but having spoken about them to the unicorn, they've taken on new significance. Now I've got some thoughts to hang on to, not like before when it was more like dealing with a slippery bar of soap in the shower.

It's Saturday. Dad is making his special oatmeal pancakes. Mom wants to know if I want to go shopping for some back-to-school clothes. "You can't wear those barn clothes to school. We could go to Fifth Street," she says smiling in a way she must consider enticing. Mostly it just makes me feel sorry for her. I mean, doesn't she have a life outside of me and Dad and work?

I put down my fork, then pick it up again and push a triangle of pancake through a puddle of maple syrup. I have so much on my mind, clothes don't seem important. Even at the best of times I don't enjoy shopping for clothes unless they're for riding. I don't know what's fashionable and I don't know what suits my body. Usually I let my mom take charge because Mom loves fashion, though she doesn't necessarily know what kids are wearing so she asks the clerks in the store. She likes to take me to the boutique clothing stores on Fifth Street and tends to push me into more adult styles, which is no easy feat given my body-of-an-eight-year-old. So in this sense, Mom is shoving me into adulthood, but on the other hand she's treating me like a baby who can't pick out her own clothes. The confusion is enough to put me off my breakfast.

Dad slips another pancake from the frying pan onto my plate. "What's the matter, Munchkin? Eat up. You don't have to go shopping if you don't want to. I see a Sears catalogue came last week, you can pick out some new clothes from that if you want."

I close my eyes, trying to analyze what Dad said, and also prepare myself to get caught in the crossfire over the cost of new school clothes if I don't quickly change the focus.

"I'm not looking forward to going back to school, that's all," I say.

"Oh, Honey, why not?" says Mom. "You always do so well. And you'll have new teachers. It'll be exciting, won't it, Tony?"

"You betcha," says Dad. He slathers butter on his pancakes and pours syrup until it flows off all sides of the stack. If I did this they'd kill me.

"Maybe there'll be new kids to make friends with," says Mom.

I shrug. I picture Amber and Topaz and feel sick. All those names they have for me, pygmy chimp being the worst. And here I am, no taller than when I left school in June. I am in desperate need of mare pee.

"When do I see the pediatrician again?" I say. My parents exchange a startled look. "I mean, what point is there in buying new clothes if I'm going to start taking Premarin and then I begin developing?"

"Oh I don't think it will happen that quickly, Honey," says Mom.

Dad checks his watch. "Yikes. I'm going to miss my tee time." He ruffles the top of my head as he bounds from the table. "I'll let you two girls figure this out."

"Girls?" says Mom, but he's already down the hall, out of earshot. She sighs then smiles stiffly. "Oh well. At least this means we're not stuck with the close-outs and over-stocks from the Sears catalogue."

I swallow some pancake. I need to build up my strength. I want to ride Brooklyn today, though apparently this will have to wait until after the shopping trip.

Mom pats my hand. "We'll have some fun. I know how important it is for teenagers to feel like they fit in, Honey."

I grunt. As though I'd like to fit in with jerks like Amber and Topaz.

"Connections with peers are very important at this stage of your life," says Mom.

I groan inwardly. In a way it's nice to have a change from the usual puberty lectures, but the teaching tone is the same.

"It's much like being in a herd," says Mom.

My mom is being so lame but she's also trying hard. "Okay, Mom. I get it."

But there's something else I understand suddenly. I've been thinking about Amber and Topaz as aliens or adversaries, but there is another way of looking at them. Along with me they are members of a herd. Granted, it's a different herd than the one I belong to with Kansas and Dr. Cleveland, but it's a herd nonetheless, with dynamics and ebbs and flows of power and influence.

Now I'm cooking.

CHAPTER FIFTEEN

I can see the sweat bead up on my mom's forehead as she cranks the ignition on the car. Getting to town to shop for clothes isn't important to me, and I'm not keen on the new plan to check in on Taylor on the way either. But Mom is going to drop me at the barn when this is all done, so for that reason I really need the car to start.

"You can do it, Mom," I say, encouragingly, the way a good boss mare would.

"I hope I haven't flooded the bloody thing."

"If you had electronic fuel ignition like Dad has in his SUV this wouldn't happen."

I guess I shouldn't have said this because Mom slaps the steering wheel with her free hand and turns open-mouthed to say something that I anticipate will not be pleasant. But I resist the urge to shrink into the seat to hide from the blast; instead I take a deep breath and square my shoulders, the way Kansas tells me to steady myself when I ride. And then the engine catches.

Mom slips the car into gear and clears her throat. "When did you learn about electronic fuel ignitions, Pumpkin?" she asks sweetly.

"Kansas told me," I say warily. I'm not sure about

quoting Kansas on yet another topic, but Mom nods encouragingly so I continue. "Kansas wants a newer truck, hers is old and it doesn't always start easily either. She says it's because it's a Ford. She wants a new Tundra but can't afford one. She says the latest models have better towing capacity. They come in four wheel drive which she says we need in our climate if you have a long driveway like she has. Unless you drive a car. In which case all wheel drive would be sufficient."

"Hmmm," says Mom, obviously having lost interest. "Honey, I bought a get-well present for Taylor. It's on the back seat. I know she's redecorating and I found the sweetest little angel mobile."

I'd forgotten the redecoration project, cut short by our biking accident.

"It's too bad she outgrew the unicorns though. I always kind of liked them," says Mom. "You must have liked them too, Sweetie, being equines."

"I dream about unicorns." I don't know why I say this. I'd certainly never planned to confess something so stupid.

"No kidding," says Mom. "I used to dream of unicorns too!"

Well that's a surprise. But kind of nice too.

Then she ruins it by going all academic on me. "Perhaps dream content is genetic too. I'll have to do a literature search."

I slouch in the seat. She is so hopeless.

"When did you start having unicorn dreams, Honey?" She doesn't even wait for me to answer, not that I was going to. "I think I started in my adolescence. And they went on for years and years." She stares off over the horizon and almost misses the turn to Auntie Sally's. "As a matter of fact, now I remember, I stopped having them when I was pregnant with you. Isn't that something?"

I grunt.

"So it has to be hormonal. This is so interesting," says Mom.

I wish I'd never brought it up.

Fortunately we have arrived at Auntie Sally's. "We'll have to talk about this more later," says Mom.

"Oh right," I say. I try not to sound sarcastic.

As usual their dog Bunga has met us on the driveway. He's leaping all over the driver-side door while Auntie Sally yells at him from the front steps. The last time Bunga did this to my dad's car, Dad said the mutt was having a near-death experience and if he did it one more time he'd kill him with his bare hands. Auntie Sally promised to take him back for more obedience classes but I guess she hasn't done it yet. She's probably been too busy. My cousins are what my mom calls "a handful". Especially Erika who is ten and gets whatever she wants, and Stephanie who is eighteen and gets everything she wants as well as things she doesn't want, like Chlamydia. In the middle is Taylor who now, thanks to me, is an invalid.

Auntie Sally ushers me to the patio out back where she says everyone is having a little picnic. My mom says she'll follow me out in a minute, which I don't believe.

Taylor looks like she's the only one who is happy to see me.

"Oh look, it's Evel Knievel," says Stephanie. She's wearing denim short shorts and a Madonna-like corset thingy. I hate it when she dresses like this. She's even worse than Amber who mostly just wears super-tight things and has bra straps hanging out all over the place. Stephanie is much more into exposure. It's bad enough in cooler winter months, but in the summer I never know where to look. What makes it worse is that I am slightly curious about what could happen to me development-wise after I start hormone treatments. Not that I'd like to turn out like Stephanie, or if I did I would have to be more modest about it, because I wouldn't want people looking, or struggling not to look like I do. I force myself to keep my eyes off her chest. There's a big tattoo on her left shoulder. I can't quite make out what it is, but clearly there are fangs.

"Evil who?" says Erika. Erika is holding a small mirror in her left hand. With her right she is using a pen to draw what could possibly be a black widow spider on her left shoulder.

"He was a daredevil stunt rider. Like our cousin here," says Stephanie. She sprawls on the lounge chair with one leg over the arm rest. "But he only ever maimed himself. He never endangered innocent passengers."

I look over my shoulder for my mom. I could use some reinforcements. But all I hear is the coffee bean grinder, so I know I'll be on my own for a while. I take a deep breath and lift my collar bones.

Taylor comes to my rescue. "Oh Stephanie, grow up. It wasn't Sylvia's fault. It was my fault. I made her double me on the bike."

"Hmmph," says Stephanie.

Taylor's foot is resting on a plastic lawn chair. She's wearing a huge sock so her amputation is not visible.

"How's the angel redecorating going?" I ask her.

"Stephanie's going to help Mom put up my wallpaper before she goes back to university next week. It's going to be wonderful."

"It's going to be ridiculous," says Stephanie. "Taylor, you are such a Pollyanna."

"What's a Pollyanna?" says Erika. In a way I'm glad she's here. Half the time I don't know what Stephanie's talking about either, but I sure don't want to admit it.

"It's someone who only looks at the positive side of things. As far as I'm concerned the only angels that are interesting are the fallen ones," says Stephanie.

"What's a fallen angel?" says Erika.

"They are angels who've gone astray," says Taylor. "They've made a mistake."

This sounds curiously like what the unicorn told me about why he lost his horn.

"They've had sex with humans," says Stephanie.

In slow motion I take a seat in an empty lawn chair. Oh no.

"You're kidding!" says Erika.

"They have sex and then their wings fall off," says Stephanie.

❧

We don't leave until almost lunch time. I'm in even more of a totally confused state than usual after a visit with my cousins. I don't have a headache exactly. It's more a feeling of pressure in the middle of my forehead. When I touch the spot with my fingers I swear I can feel a lump, and I swear the lump is bigger than it was yesterday.

The situation is not looking good. Here are the facts:

1. I am a hybrid.
2. I have lucid dreams about a fallen unicorn who has lost his horn.
3. Unicorns are not born with horns; they develop at adolescence.
4. I am entering adolescence and my forehead hurts.
5. My mom dreamt of unicorns until the time of my conception.

The conclusion is grave and obvious.

I have no alternative but to try to think about something else.

We've rolled down the car windows because it's so hot. If I hook an elbow up on the door a cool breeze blows into my hairless armpit.

I have to try harder not to think about adolescence.

I take a deep breath of road smells and then have to cough. At the traffic light all the cars stopped around us have their windows rolled up tight, and their passengers look a lot cooler than I feel, plus they're not breathing fumes so their lungs must be much more comfortable. I look at my mom again, see how damp tendrils of hair are stuck to the back of her neck, how her fingers grip the steering wheel, how her calf muscle tenses above her foot firmly planted on the brake pedal, how her eyes scan the traffic lights, preparing for the signal to go, no doubt praying that the car will respond and not die there in the middle of the road as has happened so many times before. I consider the sacrifice my mom is making for me. She'd probably prefer to be drinking wine with Auntie Sally. I feel guilty.

"Mom, why don't we go car shopping for you instead of

clothes shopping for me? I can go shopping later with Taylor, when her foot has healed. She has good taste in clothes."

"Oh, Cupcake, really…"

The light turns green. The car lurches and a new cloud of gasoline fumes wafts in through the windows. Someone honks behind us. The car lurches again, bounds forward, gains some momentum and then the engine dies. Mom frantically pumps the gas pedal to no effect, then flicks on the emergency flashers and steers the coasting car into the bike lane on the right side of the road. She rests her forehead on her hands gripped at the top of the wheel.

"Mom, it's a sign," I say, surprising even myself. I don't believe in signs. Taylor is the one who believes in signs and the influence of the spirit world. Ugh.

Mom shakes her head. "Not now, Sylvie."

A car pulls in ahead of us but does not stop. I watch as it turns in the next driveway and winds its way through a parking lot jammed with shiny vehicles and stops in a space in front of a double-door marked "Reception". Perhaps not a sign, I think. Perhaps more an opportunity. I unbuckle my seat belt, slide forward and turn to face my mom. My shoulders are square and I lift my sternum. A stream of cars whizz by. In the rear window of the last one are Amber and Topaz, laughing, pointing and making monkey faces. But even this sight is not enough to throw me from my task. Boss mare, I tell myself.

"Yes, Mom. Now. You shouldn't have to just make do—it's not fair. You deserve air conditioning. You deserve a better car."

"It's not about deserving, Cookie. You know this. It's about whether we can afford a new car." She retrieves her purse from the back seat and scrabbles through it. "Oh no. I left the cell phone on the charger. We'll have to find a pay phone."

"A pay phone? There are no pay phones around here, Mom." I focus on being patient. I want my mom to figure this out herself if she can. I don't want to bully her into it, like Hambone would do. I will be subtle, like Electra.

Mom checks the rear view mirror. "Maybe someone will stop."

"No one's going to stop, Mom. The road is too busy."

"Well I have to call the Automobile Association somehow." I see her look around and somehow fail to notice the obvious.

"Mom, we can get out here and walk to the nearest business. They'll let us phone. Or something." I indicate over my shoulder. Finally Mom picks up the cue and stares across the verge at the glass and chrome building beckoning from the other side of the parking lot.

I'm ready with an innocent blank expression when her gaze slides back to me.

"The Toyota dealership," says Mom.

I nod.

"How did you manage this?"

I shrug.

Mom slips her purse over her shoulder. "Well, we can ask to use their phone, but that certainly doesn't mean we have to buy anything."

"Sure, Mom."

A salesman holds open the door for us and we step into the air-conditioned show room. The windows are all darkly tinted. When the door closes behind us the space feels like a sanctuary from all the noise and stink of the outside world. Instead the air is full of the scent of new cars and coffee and the sound of pop music. Near the door, dark leather couches surround a coffee table strewn with shiny colourful brochures.

The salesman says his name is Ted. My mom explains that our car has broken down and we need to phone the Automobile Association. Ted suggests we take a seat and he'll bring a cell phone, and anything else we might need. A coffee perhaps? He is really nice.

"Have you got anything cold?" I ask.

"I'll see," says Ted.

"Nothing with a lot of sugar," says Mom. "Or caffeine."

"Maybe a beer then?" says Ted, winking at me.

I smile but Mom glares at both of us.

"I'll see what I can find," says Ted.

I flop into a seat beside my mom, and just about disappear into the couch. I'm feeling so much better. Things are going okay. I'm cooling off, my head feels fine and I'm in control of my thoughts. I clamber out of the depths of the couch and perch on the edge of the seat. I reach forward with one finger and slide the top brochure off the pile on the table and stuff it in my pocket. It's all about Tundra pickups. I'm taking it for Kansas. The next pamphlet shows a picture of an SUV just like Dr. Cleveland's. Under the photo, print-ed in bold letters is *Toyota Hybrids and Crossovers*. I groan. I can't get away, no matter what I do. And it's bad enough to be thinking about hybrids again but *crossovers* reminds me of the hermaphrodite barnacles I used to have as pets. For a while I thought I might be a hermaphrodite as well. In retrospect, those were the good old days. As difficult as it might have been to be a hermaphrodite, being a hybrid is much more complicated.

"What's the matter, Honey?" says Mom.

"Nothing. They've got hybrids, that's all," I say.

"Hybrids are great," says Ted, handing Mom a cell phone. "They're the way of the future. And you can reduce your family's carbon footprint."

"You don't say," says Mom.

Ted hands me a bottle of bright yellow Gatorade. "The label says it's lemon-lime." His expression is doubtful. "Though I know it looks kind of like hoss . . . "

"Thank you very much," interrupts Mom. "It's full of electrolytes, a very good choice on a hot day like today."

Great. The air-conditioning has revived my mom enough to get her back into lecture mode.

Mom checks the number on the card in her wallet and phones the Automobile Association, but for some reason they are having a busy day and won't be able to send anyone for two hours.

"I'll phone your father," she says, punching in the number.

"But he's golfing," I remind her. "He says he always turns off his BlackBerry when he's on the course."

"Oh right." But Mom has already completed the number and before she can hang up, through the tiny speaker comes my dad's voice.

"Tony?" says Mom, shoving the phone to her ear. "No of course you didn't recognize the number. Do you mean to tell me you screen your calls on the golf course and only take the ones that aren't from your family?"

Ted gives me a little smile then strolls away and stands

surveying the huge car lot. I expect he's still in ear shot though. I place a hand on my mom's arm and say loudly, "Mom, tell him you need a new car."

"I am not spying on you," says Mom into the phone. "It's an emergency, the car. . . . No, no, we're both fine, but the car has died, it's off the side of the road . . . . Well they can't come for two hours so I thought that you . . . . No, it does not just need a new battery. I thought perhaps you could leave early and . . . . No, we can't go shopping from here, it's miles to the stores, we're here at the Toy— hello? Hello, Tony?"

She stabs the off button with a finger and slaps the phone shut. I expect the face plate to fall apart from the force, but it doesn't.

"Lose the signal?" says Ted.

"Something like that," says Mom.

I open the Gatorade and take a sip. It has a thick almost oily texture. It's not bad if you can ignore the colour. Ted was right, it does look a lot like horse pee.

Mom grabs the bottle from my hand. "I could use a swig of this myself," she says.

Ted says, "I know you didn't come in here looking for a car, but why don't you let me show you a few things anyway."

I steady my breathing and wait. I know I could jump in and say, "What's the harm in looking", which wouldn't be subtle at all. Waiting is better. My mom takes another sip from the bottle. Her face transforms. She almost looks like another person. Peaceful, like after her visualization exercise, but also determined.

"What a good idea," says Mom.

She is reminding me of qualities I have seen in Kansas and Dr. Cleveland, qualities that of course I had attributed to their membership in the herd of horsewomen. But now I see it in my mom. Some sort of resolve. Perhaps it's something that comes with membership in a more general herd of women whether they are horse-nuts or not. Perhaps it comes with estrogen.

My mom places the bottle on the table and picks up a brochure. I feel a sudden rush of pride in her that I don't remember feeling before. I guess it's usually my dad I feel proud of.

Estrogen definitely has some things going for it. I wish I could have some of it for myself. Too bad I can't just drink it up, like a bottle of Gatorade. Instead I have to wait for whenever the adults decide I can have my prescription for Premarin.

I stare at the sweating half-empty bottle.

And am struck by yet another opportunity.

A pink glow has come to my mom's cheeks despite the cool air of the show room. "I don't suppose any of these come with all wheel drive," she says to Ted.

CHAPTER SIXTEEN

Mom says she's too tired to take me clothes shopping after buying her new Prius, but I think she's too excited. She drops me off at the stable then heads off to pick up Auntie Sally and take her for a spin.

Kansas isn't in the barn and her truck isn't in its usual parking space in the yard.

Brooklyn is in a small paddock off his box stall. Electra is out in the pasture with Hambone and Photon, but she's ignoring them. Instead she is standing at the fence staring at Brooklyn. Her tail is up and to one side. She pees every few minutes. She's in season and I'm in luck.

Kansas told me that often bringing a new horse onto a property will trigger the resident mares to go into season. They become totally disgusting flirts. Kansas says it's all due to hormones and the mares can't help themselves, which I suppose explains why Electra is acting so lovey-dovey about Brooklyn when she didn't even like him before yesterday.

I take one of Kansas's good stainless steel pails from the feed room out to the pasture. As soon as Electra realizes there's no food in the bucket she completely ignores me and returns to mooning over Brooklyn. I only have to wait about a minute and a half before she spreads her hind legs and pees again. I catch a cup or so before she gets annoyed with me and trots off.

It stinks. It's yellow and frothy and smells to high heaven. But it's mare urine, and it's full of hormones. I take it back to the barn, mix half of it with the remains of my Gatorade and stuff it in the fridge in the tack room. If it's cold enough and I'm thirsty enough, I know I'll be able to drink it. Maybe small amounts at a time. A sip a day, so that by the time school starts I'll be on the road to being a new woman. I'm thankful I have the refrigerator at the barn to use. Once I stored some salt water for my barnacles in the fridge at home and Mom drank it by mistake. I wouldn't want to make that mistake again. Just to be sure I use a black marker to write my name on the label. Kansas has a barn rule that we don't borrow other people's stuff without permission.

I want to wash the remains out of the bucket before Kansas gets home, but Brooklyn is watching me with such interest that I take the pail over to his paddock. It won't quite fit through the rails so I open the gate and slide in with him. Kansas told me not to get close to him unless there was a wall or a fence between us, but I think she's totally misread the situation with Brooklyn. She doesn't understand that he only bites people if they are disrespectful to him, which is completely reasonable as far as I am concerned. And I sure don't disrespect him. We're both hybrids. He may even know this already because animals are highly perceptive.

He stuffs his head in the bucket, lifts it out again and flips up his lip like he's laughing.

I squat by the bucket, looking up at silly Brooklyn,

the sun behind his head, and something strange happens to my field of vision. It's as though a shadow crosses over it, almost as if there's a blind spot in the middle. I hold my hand above my head and slowly slide it into view. There's something wrong. There's a piece missing. I blink really hard. I have to do this three times, and then I can see properly again. Brooklyn is watching me. He's lost interest in the bucket and instead is sniffing my hair. I feel his bristly nose wiggling against my scalp.

"Sylvia!"

It's Kansas. I didn't hear her drive up. Maybe it's not just my eyes playing tricks on me. Maybe my ears are packing it in too. Her truck makes almost as much noise as my mom's ex-car—how I missed her coming in the driveway is beyond me.

I stand up quickly, knocking over the bucket accidentally on purpose. Brooklyn sniffs the spill spot and does his smiley thing again.

Kansas holds open the gate for me. "You shouldn't be in there with him like that. He could take the top of your head off."

"He's smiling."

"No he's not. It's called a Flehman response. He's drawing scent molecules or pheromones towards a chemical receptor in the roof of his mouth. What was in the bucket?"

"Some Gatorade." I hate myself. I am lying to Kansas. But it's for a crucial cause.

"Odd," says Kansas. "Oh well, sometimes they do that when they smell something they haven't come across before. Come see what I got." She heads off to her truck, cooling in a patch of shade by the barn. On the front seat is a cardboard pet caddy.

"A kitten?" I gasp. "I've always wanted a kitten! But of course with my dad's allergies . . . ."

A whimpering sound emerges from the box, and a wet black nose seeks to escape through one of the round ventilation holes.

"A puppy," says Kansas. "I've always wanted a dog. Now that I'm finally not renting I can have one." She reflects for a moment. "Though a cat would be a good idea too, something to keep the mice under control in the feed room. Maybe next week you and I can go back to the shelter and look for one." She opens the caddy and lifts out a black and tan fuzzball with a round pink tummy.

"She looks like a baby bear!" I say.

Kansas cuddles the puppy in her arms. I've never ever seen her look so happy. "Her name's Bernadette," she says. And before I can say anything about what a silly name that is, she adds that this was her mom's name. "The folks at the shelter think she's German shepherd. Mostly. I don't care. Mutts are good. Hybrid vigor you know."

I cough. "Hybrid vigor?"

"Yeah. Hybrids don't have all the health problems that purebreds have. Hip dysplasia, skin problems, that sort of thing. Hybrids are tough little monkeys, right Bernadette?" Bernadette squirms and licks her ear. "I'll go put her in a stall," she says, carrying her into the barn.

Hybrid vigor. I like that. Of course I also like what the Toyota pamphlet had to say about hybrids: they are a seamless blend of the power of gas with a high voltage battery to optimize power, performance and fuel efficiency and still have 70% fewer emissions.

I am the wave of the future—vigorous, seamless, powerful and environmentally friendly. Top that, Amber.

"Hey, who's this coming?" says Kansas as a cloud of dust is stirred up where the driveway meets the road.

It takes me a second to recognize the vehicle. "It's my mom's new car."

"Nice red."

"Barcelona red metallic," I tell her. "The interior is bisque."

"Wow. But who's driving? That's not your mom."

"Oh god. It's my cousin Stephanie." I can't believe Mom let Stephanie drive her brand new car. Taylor says that Stephanie is relentless and impossible to resist, but my mom is not only an adult but also a trained helping professional. I would have thought she could bring some of her skills into play here.

The car glides to a gentle stop behind Kansas's truck which, in comparison, looks like something from a junkyard. I make a mental reminder to give her the Tundra pamphlet.

My mom is in the passenger seat. Auntie Sally is in the back.

"Was that ever fun," says Stephanie bouncing out of the car.

My mom grabs the key fob. "I'll drive back," she says.

"Yeah, whatever," says Stephanie. "Anything to be out of the house and away from all the young animals." She's still wearing her denim shorts and corset top. Kansas is staring at her; I bet she thinks Stephanie is some sort of alien creature even after my mom introduces her as my cousin.

"Now take me to meet this horse of yours," says Auntie Sally.

"Well, not exactly a horse," says Kansas.

Which stops everyone in their tracks of course.

"What?" says Mom.

"He's a hinny," says Kansas. Obviously she expected everyone to know by now. She looks to me but I won't meet her eye. Then she explains to my mom and my aunt and my cousin what a hinny is. I could die.

"Oh that's rich," says Stephanie, laughing. "Grandpa bought a half-assed horse." I wish she'd shut up. Without Taylor here there's no one to stop her. Auntie Sally gave up years ago.

My mom turns to me. "Honey, you didn't say anything about this."

"I was going to," I say.

"Kansas," says my Mom, "will this be okay? Sylvie wanted a horse. Should we send him back?"

"You could send him back?" says Kansas, with much more enthusiasm than I would have liked.

"No we can't," I say. "He's fine. Maybe he can't be much of a dressage horse, but I don't care. Hybrids are the way of the future, remember Mom?"

Auntie Sally grabs my mom's arm and tugs. "Come on, Ev, let's have a look."

I lead them around to Brooklyn's paddock.

"Well, this is disappointing," says Stephanie. "He looks like a horse to me." She leans over the top rail and dangles her fingers in Brooklyn's direction. "Hey, horsey." Brooklyn ignores her. "Kind of a cute little guy, doncha think?"

I expect Brooklyn to launch himself and maybe take her arm off for me, but he doesn't. He paws at the spot where I spilled the bucket.

"Mind if I take a look around?" Stephanie asks Kansas.

"Sure," says Kansas. "But no smoking in the barn."

"Oh, Stephanie doesn't smoke," says Auntie Sally.

"Of course she doesn't," says Kansas but she watches Stephanie's departing back through slitty eyes.

Auntie Sally says, "Can I go in and pat your horse, Sylv? I brought him a carrot."

"We're not hand-feeding him right now," says Kansas, and I know what's coming and it's too late to stop her. "You have to be careful around a horse that bites."

"He bites?" says Mom. I guess Dad never told her, which is kind of a surprise. I slide in next to Auntie Sally for protection.

"He bit the transport driver," says Kansas.

"Only because—"

Kansas jumps in before I can finish, "Sylvia, it doesn't matter why he bit someone. We have to be careful around him for a while."

"Is there anything else I don't know?" says Mom.

"How about I make us all some iced tea?" says Kansas.

They send me to find Stephanie. Of course I don't want to find her, so I walk very slowly and look first in the most unlikely places such as the shavings shed and the back of the manure pile. I figure she's probably in the tack room smelling the leather and playing with the whips, and then I remember my Gatorade bottle. Someone like Stephanie wouldn't care if my name was written on it. She'd drink it anyway. She wouldn't sip it like I was planning to do. She'd glug it all down. I'm enjoying this prospect and take my time walking down the alleyway in the barn, but then I wonder what effect it might have on Stephanie to have an overdose of estrogen. I know what happens when people don't have enough estrogen, and everything I've read emphasizes how important it is to keep hormones in proper balance. Presumably people can also get into trouble if they have an excess. Maybe she'd turn into Pamela Anderson and explode out of her corset. Or maybe she'd act like a mare in season and become a disgusting flirt even with boys she didn't like. But whatever happened, it would be my fault. Everyone would blame me.

I fling open the tack room door in a near panic. She's not there. I check the refrigerator. My Gatorade is still tucked in at the back.

That's when I hear her singing. She's an awful singer. She sounds like a cat with its tail on fire.

I follow the sound to the spare stall where Kansas put her new puppy. I stretch on my toes and can just barely see over the door. Stephanie is sitting on the floor and the puppy is on her lap, stretched out, belly-side-up on her thighs. For a second I think Stephanie must be preparing her for some sort of ritual sacrifice because Bernadette is totally vulnerable and Stephanie is leaning down towards her. She stops singing or keening or whatever she's been doing, takes a deep breath, presses her lips on the puppy's belly and blows a series of air bubbles that sound like trumpet notes, just like Auntie Sally used to do with Erika when she was a baby. Bernadette wriggles. Stephanie strokes her until she settles then she does it again.

I lose my balance and topple against the door which rattles on its hinge.

"Who's there?" says Stephanie.

I tell her it's me. Then I slide back the latch and slink

into the stall. I don't expect Stephanie will be pleased to have been caught being gentle, sweet and affectionate.

Stephanie sets Bernadette on her feet, and the puppy turns and clambers back into her lap. Stephanie strokes her, then glares at me.

"You are a very lucky person," she says.

"I know that."

"And you owe me big-time for what you've done to my sister."

I tell her I'm really really sorry.

"I don't care how sorry you feel," says Stephanie. "What you have to do is make it right."

Stephanie terrifies me so I say the first stupid thing that comes into my head. "I would if I could, I would give Taylor one of my big toes but—"

"Don't be a moron."

Bernadette tumbles out of Stephanie's lap, waddles to a corner of the stall, squats and pees. Halfway back to Stephanie she attacks a scrap of wood and wrestles it to the ground.

"Taylor's dancing days are over," says Stephanie.

I tell her I know that.

"I'm going to be away at university. Mom is useless and Erika is too young. So you're going to have to help her find a new life to pour herself into."

"Okay, Stephanie." I will say anything to make her happy.

"I think she should take up riding," says Stephanie.

She has to be out of her mind. I knew she was weird, but this is insane. "Oh no, Stephanie, that will never work. Taylor's afraid of horses. Actually she's afraid of everything, except maybe angels. And us horse people, well, we're born this way, all of us—Kansas, Dr. Cleveland, me, we were born wanting to ride and be with horses. You can't make someone a horse person."

Stephanie stands up and dusts off her bum. Bernadette makes a bee-line for her shoes and collapses on them. Stephanie scoops her up and presses her against her cheek. "This will be a healthy atmosphere for Taylor. She'll be okay with horses once she gets to know them. I know I would have turned out differently if I'd been able to ride like I wanted to when I was a kid."

I decide not to remind her that she made Grandpa pay for plastic surgery on her nose instead. She could have had a horse. Instead she got a little ski-jump. She probably doesn't want to hear this.

Bernadette's hind feet scrabble on Stephanie's chest, pulling down the edge of her corset. Despite trying as hard as I can not to look, I see another tattoo. The letters are ornately scrolled and it takes me a few seconds to decipher them. Even then they don't make sense. "Gregory?" I say.

She follows my line of vision then hikes up her top and stares daggers at me. Maybe she expects to turn me to stone, but I'm too confused by events to comply. Auntie Sally used to be married to Uncle Gregory but I haven't seen him for years and years and no one talks about him anymore. "But he left you," I say.

"He didn't leave me, you idiot. He left my mom."

"Okay." What else can I say?

"And don't you dare tell anyone," says Stephanie. She points a finger at me. "No one else knows, so if someone mentions it, I'll know you squealed, and I'll have to kill you."

"I won't say anything!" I'm sure she means it. She looks like a killer, even though she has a puppy in her arms that is licking her neck. Psychopaths often have close relationships with animals, my mom says, because they can't manage human relationships.

"That is, if I haven't killed you already for not helping Taylor get a new life without dance." She steps towards me menacingly. I can see the tattoo on her shoulder. Definitely there are fangs, and talons and scales and feathers. It's a mess. I shudder. It must be another hybrid, but this one is some sort of monster.

"Okay! I'll help her." Though I don't know how. It's not as though I don't have enough problems of my own.

CHAPTER SEVENTEEN

So yet another day passes without my being able to ride my new horse. Mom says I have to come with her while she drops off Auntie Sally and Stephanie. Then we head home. I also miss taking my first dose of mare urine.

Dad's back from his golf game. I'm thinking he must have had a high score because he sure doesn't look happy as he bursts out the front door and meets us on the driveway.

"I've been frantic," he says. "Where have the two of you been?"

"We're fine," says Mom. "We just dropped off Sally and Stephanie."

This is like throwing gasoline on a fire. "You've been at Sally's all this time? Last I heard you were broken down at the side of the road, and then my cell phone cut out."

"I dealt with it," says Mom.

"Okay," says Dad. He takes a deep breath. "You're okay, that's what counts." He looks at the car. "That's a high-class loaner."

"It's a hybrid," I tell him and he smiles at me so I tell him, "Hybrids are the way of the future."

A suspicious expression crosses his face and takes up residence. He turns to Mom but doesn't say anything.

She tosses the car's key fob into her purse. "My father," she says, "sent Sylvie a hinny."

My dad looks puzzled but still doesn't say anything.

"A hinny," says Mom, "is a cross between a donkey and a horse."

"That's a mule," says Dad.

"Not if the mother is a donkey and the father is a stallion," I say.

"Well . . . ." says Dad. For some reason he looks like he's trying not to laugh.

"I wouldn't say what you're thinking, Studly," says Mom. She's smiling.

"That smells like a new car," says Dad.

"It is," says Mom.

I'm all prepared to tell Dad about the advantages of hybrids, but Mom says, "Not now, Honey."

"How much?" says Dad.

"It's all in my name, Tony," says Mom who then turns and strides up the sidewalk and disappears into the house.

"Dad, I don't care if Brooklyn's a hinny. I'm keeping him. I like it that he's a hybrid. Hybrids are good."

"I suspect I'll be hearing a lot to that effect in the next little while," says Dad. He opens the car door and seats himself behind the wheel. He sighs. "Nice. But don't tell her I said so."

I don't understand adults. Why can't he be happy for my mom, like I'm happy for Kansas? Maybe he needs a reminder. "Kansas got a new puppy named Bernadette. Next week I'm going to help her pick out a kitten for the barn."

"That's great, Munchkin." He looks sad. I don't get it.

"How was your golf game, Dad?"

He brightens a little. "Good. Ten over par. Would have done better, but I took that call from your mom on the eighteenth and then was worried about the two of you. I decided there was nothing I could do, so I played out the hole. But I was distracted. Double bogey."

"That's too bad, Dad."

He nods, climbs out of the car and gently closes the door. There are paw prints on the panel below the window. He turns to me accusingly. "Kansas's new dog?"

"She's a puppy, Dad. She can hardly stand up."

"Bunga," we say in unison.

Dad rubs at the smudges with his finger. "Thank god, it's just dirt. No scratches."

"During the painting process they use a positively charged primer," I tell him.

I figure that Mom and Dad are going to have a bit of a dust-up about the car, followed by a make-up in their bedroom, and then later, if I'm lucky, maybe we can go out for pizza for dinner. I head off to my bedroom and shut the door so I hear as little as possible of the inevitable process.

I thumb through my Greenhawk Equestrian Supply catalogue and my Pony Club manual but somehow they don't appeal. I scan my bookcase and pull down a large hardcover that Auntie Sally found for me two years ago at the Salvation Army thrift store. I haven't looked at it for ages. I sit on the floor with my back against my bed and flip open the cover. It's all about equestrian three-phase eventing in England. The first phase is dressage, which is what Kansas loves so much, kind of like the compulsory figures phase of international figure skating. The second phase is cross-country jumping and the final phase is stadium jumping.

I skim through the dressage photos which are pretty, but when I reach the cross-country section I study each page with great care. The riders wear protective vests as well as crash helmets. The horses have protective boots on their pasterns. Some of the horses have white grease smeared on their chests so if they hit a jump they slide off, because these jumps don't fall down like the stadium ones. They are big and solid and fantastically exciting. They remind me of the dreams I have where I'm riding and it feels like I'm flying across the countryside and then I reach a fence and soar over that. I feel my heart beating faster just by thinking about it. This is what I want to do. Dressage is interesting and it can be beautiful, but it's not where my heart is. I wonder if I can explain this to Kansas. She's not that keen on jumping. When I've tried talking to her about it in the past she just said that ninety percent of a jump course is on the flat so I better improve my dressage.

I wonder if Brooklyn likes jumping. I wonder how old I will have to be before I can move to England and take up three-phase eventing.

Out in the hall I hear Mom and Dad's bedroom door snick shut. They are trying to be quiet but as usual they aren't very good at it.

My attention drifts back to the book open on my lap and then floats away again. I find myself staring in an unfocussed way through my bedroom window. The sun is still streaming in. When I change my focus to the ceiling of my room I see the funny shape again, like a shadow, or maybe a gap in my vision. This must be what it would be like if you had a horn growing out of your forehead. I raise my hand and curl my fingers around the space where a horn would be and imagine what it would feel like. Cool and smooth. Such a wonderful thing. Imagine how everyone at school would respect me if they knew I was part-unicorn. I touch my forehead with my index finger, and it's still sensitive, and the lump is still there. I'm sure it's bigger.

Behind me on top of my bookcase is my new riding helmet, but I dig out my old one from under my bed. I stand in front of the mirror hanging on the back of my bedroom door. I hold my fist gently against my forehead where my horn would be and slide on my old helmet. There's not quite enough room.

I slip down to my dad's work room for a carving tool. Technically speaking I'm not supposed to use them. Dad says they're not toys and they are very sharp and I'm sure to cut a finger off, but I know he's being over-protective. If I'm very careful everything will be fine. Of course I know they're not toys. Besides, what I'm doing is serious.

Back in my room I pull back the fabric liner of my helmet then shave away at the shell. Kansas has told me that I have to be careful with the helmet and that even dropping it could impair its structural integrity. Obviously this one is toast having been in a crash with me, but this makes it perfect to practice on. I want to see if a half-moon arch in the middle of the front brim does any harm. I shave away slivers of Styrofoam. When I'm finished I flip the liner back into place and examine my handiwork. It's great. No one would know except me.

I take my new helmet from my bookcase and repeat the surgery on this one. It goes faster because now I know what I'm doing.

I'm in Dad's work room, tucking away the blade, when Mom calls from the kitchen. We're going out for pizza.

CHAPTER EIGHTEEN

I'm dreaming, and I know I'm dreaming even though there are no horses and thankfully no unicorn.

I'm at school. I'm sitting in an empty classroom and the bell is ringing. I cringe. The last people I want to see are Amber and Topaz. I'm not ready to deal with them yet, I haven't started my estrogen treatment. My boss mare techniques have not been mastered.

I hear footsteps in the hall. The door handle turns.

And I remind myself: this is a lucid dream. I can make it do whatever I want. Who would I like to see? I surprise myself so much with my answer that I almost wake up, but I steady myself and in walks Logan Losino.

He hasn't grown over the summer either. He looks exactly the same as he did in June. He has nice eyes and he's not very big, though of course he's taller than me.

He smiles when he sees me and sits in the desk beside mine.

"Funny meeting you here," he says. "You come here often?" Logan Losino has always been quite the jokester.

"Usually I'm riding," I tell him. "Usually I try to avoid school."

"I don't blame you. Amber and Topaz." He rolls his eyes. They're blue.

"I thought you liked them."

"That's not who I like." He tilts his head and gives me the saddest look I have ever seen in my life.

I don't know what to say.

"Amber and Topaz aren't nice," he tells me, as if I don't know that. "And they're not smart. They're not funny. They don't care about other people."

"So why do you hang out with them all the time?"

"Someone has to keep them under surveillance," he says.

Wow. What a guy. He's sacrificing himself for the good of the community. "Logan Losino, you would have made one heck of a boss mare if it weren't for the fact that you're missing some ovaries," I tell him. He looks disappointed so I add, "Of course I may not have ovaries either, being an infertile hybrid, but this won't stop me from being a boss mare." Which actually puts me into a flurry of confusion as I think about how a woman can be a woman without ovaries or even secondary sexual characteristics, and how a unicorn can be a unicorn if its horn has fallen off. But as much as I stretch definitions, I can't imagine Logan Losino as a boss mare, which seems a shame.

He is staring at my forehead. I put up a hand, and I can feel the horn.

"Cool," he says. "I wish I had one of those."

"Well you can," I tell him, and then I give him one. And after I've enjoyed feeling happy for a while, I wake myself up.

That was a great dream.

That was one of the best. Logan Losino. I've never dreamt about him before. And it's nice to know that I can bring someone into one of my lucid dreams without something bad happening to them.

If only it was as easy to grant wishes in the real world as it is in the world of lucid dreaming. Which reminds me of all the work ahead of me. There are so many things that I decide to make a plan. Of course, some of it I have to put in code in case Mom finds it.

1. Continue to work on becoming a boss mare (the "Gatorade" project).

2. Remind Mom (again) to get me an appointment with the pediatrician.

3. Make Kansas understand that my equestrian goal is to learn how to jump.

4. Deal with Stephanie's request that I find a way of making Taylor into a horse woman (more "Gatorade"???)

5. Brooklyn . . . .

I don't know what to write about Brooklyn. I know he's my responsibility, and I know I want to train him, and I want to learn to ride him, but somehow I don't know how to put this into a plan. It's like whatever I have to do with Brooklyn is still up in the air somehow, whirling around over my head.

Even though I don't exactly believe in the spirit world, I find myself thinking about what the unicorn told me. Not only can I bring people from the real world into my lucid dreaming world, but I can also take things from the dream world into the real world. Maybe there are things I can do before I am a full-fledged boss mare.

I'm getting ready to leave for the barn when Dr. Tanya Bashkir phones. I tell her my mom and dad have left for work already but she says it's me she wants to talk to about the samples she took from Brooklyn's forehead. I am so wonderstruck at being treated like a responsible adult that at first it's difficult to concentrate on what she has to say. She thinks Brooklyn has some sort of dermatitis, but it's nothing she's ever seen before. (With everything that's been happening lately, this doesn't surprise me). She says the lab was unable to cultivate anything as they could with regular bacteria, and nothing showed up under the microscope until they did some special staining. He has some sort of spirochete infection. (She spelled it out for me and I wrote it down so I could tell Kansas). She doesn't think it's contagious. I've never heard of spirochetes before. Tanya says they come in several forms, one of the more common being syphilis, and of course I've heard of that one.

"So does he need to be on antibiotics?" I ask.

"I'm not sure what he needs," says Tanya. "But I've made up a solution for you to try. I've had some success with it in the past on horn loss in cattle."

I almost drop the phone.

"A cow's horn can fall off?" I ask, though I'm not sure I want the answer. I find it very disturbing considering what a fallen cow might have done to deserve its fate.

"It's a foot problem," says Tanya. "Horn refers to the hoof capsule."

This is slightly comforting but I don't have any time to relax because the next thing she says is, "I don't run into many cross-species contaminations."

Another cross-over. Why can't my life be simple?

I'm mulling everything over, wondering what question I could possibly ask that wouldn't sound totally bizarre, when Tanya pipes in to say she'll drop the solution at the barn when she passes by today. Then she wants to know how Brooklyn and I are getting along. I tell her I haven't ridden him yet.

"Well there's lots of time," she tells me.

I tell her I've decided I want to do three phase eventing but I'll have to wait until I can move to England.

"Why would you have to move to England? There's a great cross-country course two hours down the highway."

I could hug her. I could squeeze myself through the phone line, pop out the other end, and throw my arms around her.

Then she brings me back to earth. "You'll have to see if Brooklyn likes it though. Being a hinny, he's more intelligent than most horses. If he doesn't like jumping cross-country or finds it too scary or dangerous or difficult, it won't be any fun for either of you. It's a very ambitious and demanding sport, for both horses and riders."

"Kansas says domestic horses have a job to do and that basically they have to get with the program."

"I don't disagree with her entirely," says Tanya. "But hybrids like hinnies and mules aren't the same as horses. They have to be handled differently. They won't be bullied."

I'm thinking I should explain the difference to her between bullies and boss mares, except that as I try to put my words together I'm not sure I know the difference, other than subtlety, which doesn't seem enough somehow. Suddenly it seems that in both cases it's basically a matter of getting your own way. Somehow this doesn't sit right with me. Could I have this whole boss mare thing all wrong?

"There's something else you need to be aware of in dealing with Brooklyn," continues Tanya. "I've seen it in handling mules. I haven't worked with many hinnies but I assume hinnies will be similar. You'll have found that with horses their two main reactions to stress are fight or, more commonly, flight. Mules have another one: if they're really frightened, they'll freeze. That's why some people call them stubborn, but they're not really. I had to work on a mule once and the procedure was a bit, well, unpleasant. I asked him to move and it was like he was frozen to the spot, but when I leaned my shoulder in against his chest I could feel his heart pounding like a jackhammer."

"Fight, flight or freeze," I say, remembering how Brooklyn hadn't wanted to leave the horse trailer.

"Right. And you have to learn to read their expressions, which are different from horses. You don't get the little tail-swish warning, or a semi-pinned ear. Everything can look just fine, and then—whammo."

"Like when Brooklyn bit the truck driver," I say.

"Exactly. Hinnies aren't horses. They're hybrids. You've got lots to learn and Kansas won't be able to help you with all of it. Just a minute."

I hear muffled voices at the other end, then Tanya comes back on the line and says there's an emergency call and she has to hit the road, which is just as well because she's given me too much to think about already.

I won't be able to count on Kansas. Already I can't count on my mom and dad. They know nothing about equines that I haven't taught them. And Grandpa is too easily confused.

I'm on my own. This is exciting and terrifying at the same time. I rub my forehead, where my horn would be or will be, and I feel better. I can do this. I know I can. I am a hybrid, and hybrids are the way of the future. Hybrids have vigor.

I put on my new riding helmet and pedal off to the farm. When I get to the top of the driveway I can see Auntie Sally's car in the parking area. Auntie Sally is supposed to be at work. Then I see the skid marks where the car braked, and I know Auntie Sally would never drive this fast. Stephanie must have been at the wheel.

I think about turning around and pedaling back home, but she'd only come looking for me.

She's not in the car. I find her in the barn, and she's brought Taylor, who is on crutches. Braveheart's head is out over his stall door and he's snorting and blowing like a wild thing as they pass by. I guess he's never seen a one-legged person on sticks before.

Before I can warn them about Brooklyn, they're at his stall. Brooklyn leans his head out over the door and sniffs Taylor's hand. I figure she's about to lose another digit but there's not much I can do about it. You don't run in barns, and you don't scream. It just upsets everybody. So I walk as fast as I can, and by the time I get there it's obvious that Brooklyn likes Taylor. But the really amazing thing is that Taylor seems to like Brooklyn too. She must still be on drugs, otherwise she'd be afraid. She's afraid of everything unless it's made of gauze and sprinkles. I don't mean to be unkind, it's just true.

"Hey," I say behind them.

"Hey Evel," says Stephanie.

Taylor doesn't answer. She's mesmerized by Brooklyn's nose. "You're so soft," she says. She lowers her cheek to Brooklyn's nostril. A few strands of her hair waft up when he exhales.

"Taylor, I wouldn't do that if I was you," I warn her.

"He's so sweet," says Taylor.

I look at Stephanie, hoping for a clue about Taylor's personality change. "Is she still on medication?" I whisper.

"Tylenol 3's," says Stephanie aloud. So I guess we can talk about it openly.

"Maybe I should take some of those for my first day of school," I say without thinking, leaving myself wide open to some sarcastic comment from Stephanie.

But she surprises me. "School sucks," she says. "That's why family has to stick together."

Ah. Her campaign. I understand. Our eyes meet and I hold her gaze. "Okay, Stephanie," I tell her.

Meanwhile Taylor has opened the stall door and hopped in to Brooklyn's stall, her crutches held in one hand.

"Oh that's really not a good idea . . . ," I say. But Brooklyn is sniffing the crutches curiously, not like Braveheart would. Obviously Brooklyn is not worried that crutches are some kind of horse torturing device. He lips the butterfly nut at the hand rests but doesn't offer to bite anything. He drops his head and sniffs the rubber end on one crutch, then his nose drifts over to examine Taylor's bandaged foot. When he's finished, and this takes him forever (during which time I have died and come back to life several times as I worry that he's going to rip the bandage right off and then stomp Taylor to death in front of our very eyes which will give Stephanie the excuse she's been looking for to offer me as a ritual sacrifice to whatever pagan gods she worships) he lifts his head, and rests it gently on Taylor's shoulder.

"He likes me," says Taylor.

Stephanie looks at me and gives me a grin which I find kind of menacing. I'm feeling pretty overwhelmed.

"My dad won't go for this," I say. "He won't pay full board for a horse if I'm sharing."

"Your dad is such a Neanderthal," says Stephanie.

There's no room for compromise with Stephanie. There never is. I have to find a way of coping with the situation.

"Just a minute," I say. And I beat a retreat to the tack room. I open the fridge and pull out my jar of Gatorade mixed with Electra pee. Electralytes, I tell myself, hoping a joke will make it taste better. I twist off the cap. I take a sip, a very very small one, hoping mare urine will work like homeopathic remedies where you only need a molecule or two to be effective, which would be great because truly it tastes foul. But it's worth it. I instantly feel more powerful. I can handle this. Maybe I can convince my dad. Maybe I can keep taking lessons on Electra so my riding doesn't deteriorate too much. Maybe Kansas will let me ride Hambone. Because it seems my destiny is to be hanging around with a hinny and Taylor while I help put her life back in order. And this hardly seems like bullying boss mare activity. It feels more like being a herd leader.

I go back to make a deal with Stephanie and Taylor. And, as it seems necessary, with Brooklyn.

Kansas is standing at the stall door. She's holding Bernadette in her arms and she's looking at Taylor and Brooklyn with total disbelief. "Who woulda thought?" she says. She cuddles Bernadette against her chest and the puppy reaches up and licks her chin. It's weird, but I feel a bit jealous. Kansas used to take care of me, and now she's all focused on a puppy.

Stephanie says, "Sylvia wants to share Brooklyn with Taylor."

I say, "Not exactly—"

But Kansas says, "Fine with me. We talked about this in the hospital, about Taylor taking up riding instead of dancing."

"We did?" says Taylor.

"You were stoned," I tell her. And I know I would sound too selfish if I talked about how I wasn't sure I wanted to share Brooklyn, and that I wanted him all for myself. Instead I tell Kansas that I want to learn to jump, and I want to ride cross-country, because that has always been my dream.

Kansas puts Bernadette on the ground. The puppy does a staggering trot down the length of the alleyway, looking much like Brooklyn did when he was pretending to be lame. I expect Kansas to argue with me. I expect her to lecture me on how important flatwork is. Instead she says, "Electra can teach you to jump. After that we can see if Brooklyn here has any talent for it."

And Brooklyn says, "Haw haw haw."

CHAPTER NINETEEN

"Doing the right thing isn't always easy," says the unicorn.

"I know that," I tell him. "Maybe I'm just not good at sharing. Brooklyn was going to be mine. Now I see he likes my cousin best."

"And you think you owe her."

"Yeah."

We're sitting under a tree in the shade. Well, I'm sitting. The unicorn is lying down beside me. His head is on my lap. I'm stroking the bit where his horn used to be. When he stops talking he makes a kind of purring sound.

He lifts his head and looks at me with one eye. "What if you didn't owe her? What if she'd cut off her toe some other way? What if you had nothing to do with any of her problems? How would things be different?"

I think about this carefully. Without Stephanie menacing me, would I have agreed to share Brooklyn with her? And I'm surprised to realize that yes, I probably would. I guess I love Taylor. I sigh.

"This isn't over," says the unicorn.

"What?"

But before he can answer, I wake up, because the phone is ringing and ringing in the kitchen and no one else is getting up to answer it. For some reason the answering system doesn't kick in. It's on about the fiftieth ring when I pick it up.

"Oh Pipsqueak, is that you?"

"Oh hi Grandpa."

"Did I get you up? Oh blast, I forgot the time change, it must be really early out there, I'm sorry, I'll call back later and talk to your mom."

"It's okay, Grandpa. It's nice this time of day." I check the clock on the microwave. It's 5:30. I haven't been up this early in my entire life.

"I wanted to talk to your mom about how things are going with . . . er . . . your horse," says Grandpa.

"You can talk to me about that, Grandpa. I am fourteen," I remind him, in case he's forgotten again.

"Oh dear," says Grandpa. "It's just that I took Travis on a drive yesterday and we stopped by his farm. Travis is in long term care now, and he's not enjoying it very much. The food is terrible. His son is running the farm, that's his youngest son, his name escapes me right now, but it doesn't matter, it will come back to me. Not the oldest son, who's kind of a lazy-bones if you ask me, though of course Travis never says so much, but I can read between the lines. Not that I've ever really taken to the younger one either, the sneaky little bastard—"

"Grandpa?"

"Yes Pipsqueak?"

"What about Brooklyn?"

"That's what I was getting to," says Grandpa. "So when we drove up to the farm, we stopped at the house, but then Travis didn't like that and of course he still can't walk very well, so he told me to drive around to the barn. When we got there he looked out into the paddock and said, 'What's Brooklyn doing here, I thought you sent him to your grand-daughter?'"

My heart is pounding so loud I'm sure even Grandpa can hear it down the end of the phone line.

"We sent you the wrong animal," says Grandpa. "His son did it. I told him to send Brooklyn, the grey, but he sent the other grey. He said it was a misunderstanding, but we know he wanted to be rid of him. He'd been chasing the cows. Well, and the dogs, the cats, anything really. He sent you the hinny."

"Grandpa, I know that Brooklyn's a hinny. My veteri-narian told me. I don't mind. Really. Hybrids are the way of the future."

"Are you sure, Pip? Because I'd pay to have him shipped back home to Saskatchewan."

"Oh you can't do that, Grandpa. He and Taylor have bonded. Taylor's going to share him with me. It will be fine. There are more important things than my becoming an Olympic equestrian. And Kansas says I can take jumping lessons on Electra for a while."

Grandpa is silent for a long time. Then he says, "Well, Sylvia, I admire you for that, but you want to be a rider and you want your own horse. I imagine Taylor wants a pet, and the hinny will do just fine for that." He coughs, and tells me he has to put the phone down while he gets a glass of water. I'm pleased that when he comes back on the line, he remembers what we were talking about and picks up right where we left off. "I just remembered something. You and Taylor will have to be careful—Travis told me the hinny bites some people, but only if they've offended him."

"Like the transport truck driver," I remind him.

"He bit the driver?" says Grandpa. I guess he's forgotten, though this isn't the sort of thing I'd expect to slip someone's mind. Maybe he's repressed the memory—that's what Mom would say. She'd say he felt so guilty about sending me a horse that bit people, that he'd delete the memory, or at least move it to the trash bucket, like on the computer, she said, trying to make a metaphor that was understandable for me and going overboard as usual.

"Maybe I didn't tell you, Grandpa," I say, so he doesn't feel stupid.

"I think I should talk to your mom, Pipsqueak," says Grandpa. "You're a rider, I know you are. You don't want a pet."

"We can't afford to board two horses, Grandpa. And Auntie Sally doesn't have any money."

"No, she never does," says Grandpa with a big sigh. "But Travis really wants you to have this horse of his. He says he's too good a horse to be wrecked by his son. And he wants Brooklyn to enjoy the benefits of belonging to a teenage girl at least once in his life."

This confuses me for a few seconds, because I keep thinking that I already own Brooklyn, when in fact the horse named Brooklyn is still back in Saskatchewan. And then I find I can't bear to think about the possibility that my real horse, the one I was supposed to have, is still standing in field hundreds of miles away. A real horse, not a hybrid. It's too much. It makes me want to laugh and cry at the same time because I just can't see how it's possible.

"Put your mom on the phone, Pips," says Grandpa.

"She's still sleeping, Grandpa. Could you phone back in four hours or so?"

"Four hours? Hell's bells, I really got it wrong this time didn't I? But sure, I can do that Pips. You go back to bed. Don't worry about anything."

And then because I'm dying of curiosity, I ask him, "So, Grandpa, what's the hinny's real name?"

Grandpa groans. "Just a minute, it'll come to me," he says. "Travis did tell me, he said, 'Lord love a duck, they shipped . . . .' Oh it started with the letter S, I know that much, and it was a short name. Give me some time here."

I can barely stand the tension, but I say, "It's okay, Grandpa. You can tell me another time. I think Taylor likes calling him Brooklyn."

"But he knows his name, Pips, you can't go around changing names on an animal as smart as that one. It'll make him all depressed. Travis loved that hinny. He said he was like a boy on four hooves. He's a real character."

"Yeah, we know that, Grandpa. He pretended to be lame."

Grandpa barks out a laugh. "Oh Travis told me about that. He's got a few tricks up his sleeve, that one does." He starts coughing again, and drops the phone on the counter. He's gone such a long time I worry that maybe I should be calling 911, though how I could do that with the line engaged I don't really know. But then Grandpa comes back, and his voice is all scratchy from coughing, and he says, "I got it, Pips. I remember his name. It's Spike."

And I laugh, and tell him that's perfect, and I hang up the phone and go back to bed because there's someone I have to talk to about all of this before it's time to get up.

CHAPTER TWENTY

"Spike?" I say to the unicorn.

He nods his great head. "Wait until you meet the real Brooklyn," he says. "He's magnificent. Well, for a hornless one."

I look at him to see if he really hears what he said, because after all, he's hornless now too.

He notices. "It takes a lot more than a horn to make a unicorn," he says. "I'm no less a unicorn because my horn came off than you are less a woman for not having ovaries."

I consider this in silence for a while. I like the idea a lot. And then since we're being so friendly, I ask him. "Do you know how you really lost your horn?"

His head drops. "I told you already. I strayed. I sinned. I am paying the price."

"My veterinarian said something about spirochetes and cross-species contamination."

His head snaps up. "You mean it's possible I'm not being punished? I'm just infected?"

"That's what I figure."

He trots an excited small circle around me. Then he bucks and breaks to a canter and the circle gets bigger. Then he's galloping and pretty soon he disappears over a hill and all I can hear is his silly bugling, the one that sounds like he's laughing.

And it occurs to me that I may never see him again. Even though he has annoyed me, intruded in my dreams, and made me mad, I feel a great wave of sadness.

I wake up. I feel sad until I rub the sore spot on my forehead and feel the lump is still there. My mom would say I've just distracted myself but I don't think so. I think I truly feel fine.

At breakfast I remind my mom again that she needs to make an appointment for me with the pediatrician so I can start on estrogen. The sooner I can get on real medication and stop drinking Electralytes, the better. Mom tells me she'll phone first thing Monday morning. Then I tell her that Grandpa phoned and that he said he would phone her back but given his short-term memory problems, maybe she should call him instead.

"What short-term memory problems?" says Mom, and after a few seconds I see that she's kidding. Having a new car has done wonders for her. Or maybe it was the guided visualization.

"They shipped me the wrong horse," I tell her.

She looks over her shoulder to make sure Dad isn't coming down the hall, then sits down at the table with me. "They what?"

"Brooklyn's still back in Saskatchewan. They sent Spike by mistake."

"Oh no," says Mom.

"It's okay," I tell her. "Spike is going to help Taylor adjust to not being able to dance. They've bonded."

"But what about you, Sweetie? You want your own horse."

I shrug. What else can I do?

"All those dreams you have," says Mom. "About galloping and jumping." She takes my hand. I never thought she paid attention to my dreams. I didn't think she listened. I find myself getting all choked up.

"Summer's over anyway," I manage to say. "I'll be fine. And Taylor needs some help."

Mom looks doubtful and proud at the same time. She leans over and kisses me on the forehead, barely missing the sore spot, then ruins it all by saying, "It takes a person with a very strong sense of self to make a sacrifice like this."

I ride my bike to Kansas's place. Spike is in the big paddock with the other horses when I get there, though Hambone isn't letting him near the mares. He's off to the side, grazing all by himself. Kansas is giving Dr. Cleveland a riding lesson. Braveheart is pretty amazing, but I don't think he's easy to ride. When he canters, Dr. Cleveland's bum comes right out of the saddle and crashes back in again with each stride. Kansas tells her she's doing a good job though, and Braveheart doesn't seem to mind. I know if I did this on Electra she'd have a hissy fit, and who knows what Spike would do. Probably he'd reach around and rip my leg out with his teeth.

After a while I notice that Spike must have grown bored eating by himself, because he's trotting off towards the other horses. Before he can get close Hambone rounds up the girls who don't seem at all unhappy to be taken to another corner of the pasture. It's so much like how Amber and Topaz keep everyone away from me at school that I get a lump in my throat. I glare at Hambone. I want to yell at him. Then I notice that Hambone's tail is clamped tight against his bum. His ears are half-back, and I realize that he's actually afraid of Spike. There's no reason to be afraid, Spike's too small to be a threat. He's just different, that's all.

This insight puts a whole new spin on my social difficulties at school.

I wander across the yard, open the gate and slip into the paddock. For fun, I call out for Brooklyn and he doesn't even react. Then I shout, "Spike!" and he whips his head up and laughs at me. So I guess he does know his name. But he doesn't run for the gate, not like he would do if it was Taylor calling him.

I'm feeling kind of sad about everything, so I go back to the barn for a shot of Electralytes. The stuff hasn't improved with age, and Kansas finds me spitting into the sink with the bottle in my hand.

"Has that stuff gone off?" she asks grabbing the bottle from me. "You'd think they would've put enough sugar and preservatives in it to stop that." She takes a deep sniff before I can stop her. "Holy crap," she says, pouring it into the sink. I watch it swirl away down the drain, and I'd probably be feeling totally hopeless except I remember what the unicorn said about being no less a woman.

I tell Kansas what Grandpa told me about Spike, including the bit about him chasing dogs, which kind of worries me. But Kansas says this is fine. Bernadette will learn to stay out of Spike's paddock, and he can focus on keeping the place free of strays.

Dr. Cleveland comes in and puts her saddle on the rack in her locker. "That was fantastic, Kansas," she says. "The best lesson ever."

Kansas nods politely. "You're making great progress, Kelly, you'll be back in shape in no time."

"Oh do you really think so?" says Dr. Cleveland.

"Oh yes," say Kansas and I at the same time.

Kansas picks up a small white tub from the counter by the sink. "That vet dropped off this ointment for your pony's face." I can tell she still hasn't forgiven Dr. Bashkir for knowing Declan. Adults are too weird.

"It's for horn loss," I say.

"Oh, I don't think so," says Kansas.

"Unless you mean the hoof capsule," says Dr. Cleveland.

I decide not to correct them. Maybe I do have a strong sense of self.

CHAPTER TWENTY-ONE

I'm back at school, waiting for math class to begin. I can't believe the summer is over already. Also, I can't believe that I've got Mr. Brumby again as my math teacher. Amber and Topaz are both in my class, too. It only took about five seconds for Amber to point out that I didn't grow at all over the summer and that I'm still a pathetic little shrimp. I have to rub my fingers on my forehead underneath my bangs to give myself strength because I'm still waiting for an appointment with the pediatrician, and now I'm out of Electralytes.

Then Logan Losino appears and says, "Hey, Sylvia, my big brother tells me you got a horse this summer." Logan Losino is wearing some sort of knit ski cap. We won't have snow for months. It's black and pulled down so it's riding just above his eyebrows. Maybe I did do something to Logan by drawing him into my dreams. I want to see if there's a lump on his forehead too, but don't want to look like I'm staring. My heart pounds.

"Bad hair day, Logan?" says Topaz, reaching for the hat.

Of course. That's what's he's doing, he's covering up a bad haircut. What was I thinking?

Amber grabs Topaz's arm and stops her. She turns laser-eyes to Logan Losino and says, "You have an older brother?"

Logan Losino says, "Yeah, he goes out with Sylvia's cousin, Taylor Tersk."

Amber looks to me wide-eyed. "Your cousin is Taylor Tersk? She's in my dance class. She's amazing." She looks shocked, and a bit disappointed too, probably wondering if this means she won't be able to pick on me any more because of my famous cousin. Just to be safe, I decide not to say anything about my role in ending Taylor's dancing career.

But then I notice that Topaz has taken an interest in me too. She's staring at me and her eyes look like they're about to fall right out of their sockets. "You ride?" she says.

I nod. I try to make it look like I don't really care, though of course this has been my fantasy, that having a horse would make a difference to how I fit in with the herd dynamics at school.

Topaz says, "And you actually have your own horse? You don't just ride lesson ponies?"

I nod again. Nonchalant. But what I'm thinking is, can the conversion of my enemies really be this easy?

But then Amber says, "Oh no not another one. Not another smelly horse-nut."

And Topaz says, "Shut up, Amber."

I find an empty desk and take a seat. Logan Losino takes one right beside me. It must be awful to have such a bad haircut that you'd wear a ski cap on a warm day. Although this possibility is not as awful as having to wear a hat to hide a horn growing out of your forehead. I take a close look to be sure, and can't see a lump. Though with a black hat it's really hard to tell. Unlike in my dream, Logan grew taller over the summer. And he grew something else. There's a shadow of a mustache over his lip. Not dark and bristly like my dad's. It's more like the mustache my grandma used to have before she died. But still, it's a start. His features have changed too. He looks less like a little boy, though I can still see the original jokester Logan Losino lurking in the background of his face.

"How was your summer, Logan?" I say. I think it's the first time I've ever talked to him. I can't believe I'm being this brave. Maybe I don't need Premarin.

Before Logan can answer, Mr. Brumby comes in, slaps a pointer on his desk, yells at us all to be quiet, and then glares at each and every one of us in turn up and down the rows. This is what he did last year, too. He softens up over the term, though not a lot. I look up to the ceiling and for a second I think that the blind spot is there again, the one I'd have if I'd grown a unicorn horn out of the middle of my forehead. Then I realize that it's just one of the lights flickering. You'd think the custodians would have attended to this over the summer holidays. Besides, thinking I was part unicorn was a silly childish fantasy. I know that now. I don't need to believe stuff like this any more, even though I still don't know what the lump is on my forehead. Maybe it's one last after-effect of the growth hormone. Maybe I grew extra bone in my head instead of in my femurs. As long as I can get my riding helmet over it, I don't care.

Of course, I understand I'm still a hybrid though, because my mom is a psychoanalyst and, as Stephanie was so kind to point out, my dad is a Neanderthal. I can live with that.

There's a knock at the classroom door. Mr. Brumby

looks furious about having his reign of terror interrupted. To make it worse when he comes back in the room he stares directly at me and says, "Sylvia. Office. Family emergency." Then he yells at Logan Losino for wearing a hat in his classroom, but I'm out the door before I can see the haircut from hell. Or something worse.

My heart has gone crazy. My grandpa must have died. I know he talked to my mom on the phone last night and afterwards no one would tell me what it was about. Mom and Dad went directly to their bedroom and as much as I wanted to know what was going on of course I didn't listen at the door because . . . well, because of the usual way they make up when things aren't going well. Probably they wouldn't talk to me because they were too upset, and they didn't want me to worry. Now look what's happened. I never got to say goodbye. Just like with the unicorn.

Mom and Dad are both waiting for me in the office. They look so serious I think I might die myself, but they won't tell me what's happened until I get to the car.

I grab my stuff from my locker and wonder if maybe the unicorn and my grandpa are together now, running pain-free across the hills of Saskatchewan or Heaven or someplace.

I hurry on out to the parking lot. I'm looking for Dad's SUV and it's not there. Instead they've brought Mom's car, and when I climb in, there's Grandpa sitting in the back seat. And no one's looking serious any more.

"Sorry to drag you out of math class, Munchkin," says Dad.

I look from one grinning face to the other. "What is going on?" I say.

"Kansas told us to come and get you. She said this was something you wouldn't want to miss," says Mom. "We

didn't think Mr. Brumby would understand, so we . . . ."
She can't seem to finish the sentence so Dad does it for her.

"We lied," he says matter-of-factly.

Mom grimaces and squeezes her eyes shut for a couple
of seconds, then sighs and presses the start button.

"I flew out specially for this," says Grandpa. "Used up
all my frequent flyer points."

I am totally and completely lost.

A cell-phone ringer sounds, from the speakers in the car.

"What?" says Mom.

"Incoming!" says Dad, reaching to press a button on the
steering wheel. "Tony here," he announces.

A strange voice comes through the speakers. "Tony! It's
Brad, returning your call."

Mom's face is pink. "You programmed my car to take
your cell phone calls?"

Dad tells Brad he's in a meeting and will call him later.
"Come on, Ev, I was just playing around with your manual,
and knew you'd never use this function. Not with how you
feel about cell phones and driving." Then he swivels in his
seat so he can see me.

"There's a transport truck coming in from Saskatchewan," he says. "The driver called Kansas from the ferry."
He checks his watch with what I think is an unnecessary
flourish—he doesn't need to drag things out like this.
"They'll be here in an hour."

"Tony . . . " says Mom.

Grandpa leans over and whispers to me, "Dakota said
you'd want to be there when he unloads."

And finally I get it. "The real Brooklyn?" I say.

And he nods.

ACKNOWLEDGMENTS

Writing may be an isolating endeavor for some, but my books always seem to me to be products of a wonderful community effort. I owe my friends and family for their continued support, encouragement and tolerance.

In particular, I would like to thank the following:

Annette Sharp and Kojack for the long-ears help.
Mark Hobby for the hoof talks.
Natasha for the joke.
Glenice Neal for the Toyota Prius test drive.
Anna, Seiko and Tomiko for their thoughtful reviews.
Isobel Springett for another fantastic photo for the cover.
Rita Picard for her artistic talent and technical wizardry on the video book trailer.
Randal Macnair and Ron Smith at Oolichan Books for believing in me and Sylvia.
And Mike, for holding it all together.

Photo: Isobel Springett

Susan Ketchen was born and raised on Vancouver Island. She has successfully pursued an alarming number of educational paths and professional careers, including over a decade in the field of marriage and family therapy. She can sometimes be found out standing in her field, and always on the web at www.susanketchen.ca.